MAGICIAN UNBOUND

DIVINATION IN DARKNESS BOOK TWO

RENÉE DES LAURIERS

For Maya

CHAPTER 1

The darkness wasn't supposed to move. Not from all those forgotten places, where it settled into cracks and crevices and behind everything. It wasn't made to overpower the light. To dull the streetlamps. To cast its web of shadows and linger.

Ryan frowned as he pulled into the Safeway parking lot, slowing his Mustang to a crawl. The entire lot was empty, and it was never empty. He always had to circle through the spaces at least twice—usually getting tricked by a spot taken by a shopping cart, or a tiny car hidden out of sight.

It was also rather darker than he remembered.

Were they even open? It was only 8:00; they were supposed to be open until 11:00. It wasn't a holiday or anything. Ryan squinted at the store windows. He could make out watermelon stacked up in a pile and a shopkeeper in a dark apron, sweeping. Clearly, they were open. Just no customers in sight.

Weird.

Ryan rolled his eyes at his phone buzzing in the cup holder. His mom was probably letting him know for the fifth time that his grandma's heirloom ring was available, or about venues he could reserve.

He'd had to get out of the house, jumping at the opportunity to pick up more pasta sauce at Safeway when he saw the first message in his mom's tirade.

When are you going to make an honest woman out of that nice girl?

It wasn't that he didn't want to marry Sonia. She checked all the right boxes. But why the rush? Things were going well. Ryan didn't see the need to rock the boat. They'd barely been dating for a year. Their one-year anniversary was just last month. It wasn't like that woman was going to back off once he was married. Oh, no. Then it was going to be *When are you giving me grandchildren?* Or *When will I get another grandchild?* Ryan wasn't sure what came after that demand, but he knew that more demands would come.

He turned the Mustang into the parking spot directly under a flickering streetlamp. The light seemed oddly dull. Yellow and strained, casting the parking lot into shadow. It felt as if the store were farther than it should have been. The light from the Safeway windows was just out of reach.

Hesitating. Ryan had to forcibly shake his head to jolt himself out of his thoughts. He rubbed the warmth out of the tips of his fingers as they paused on the door handle.

It's just Safeway. I'm just getting pasta sauce. Get your shit together, you're an adult.

Paranoid.

He rushed over to the entrance with a hurried step, all while telling himself over and over again that he was being stupid.

Inside, everything was painfully normal. The shopkeeper whom he'd seen dozens of times before, with the silver name tag "Dave," just shrugged when Ryan asked if something strange was going on.

"Just slow right now. It was pretty packed like ten minutes ago."

See. Not a big deal at all.

Just a random coincidence that they happened to be cleared out right now. Everyone was probably out watching some game on ESPN that he'd forgotten about. Or off at their kid's dance recital. Or it could have been any combination of one of the random things people did when they weren't off food shopping. Mere coincidence. Probably happened to everyone at least once in their life.

Ryan strolled into aisle seven and picked up the pasta sauce, and then two more because it was on sale... and some extra virgin olive oil. They were running low. Wouldn't hurt to grab some now. Before swinging two aisles over to see if they had more of the extra dark roast back in stock.

Nine minutes later and one hundred twenty dollars poorer, he headed back to his parking spot, fumbling for his keys, and holding two bags in one arm awkwardly.

He heard the jangle when his keys dropped to the ground.

The streetlamp gave out.

Everything plunged into shadow and Ryan squinted, trying to adjust to the pitch black. He searched for the keys, but they weren't anywhere near him.

Huh. That was annoying. Nothing but pavement wherever he reached.

Ryan patted his back pocket, feeling denim. Where was his phone? He grimaced when he remembered it was in the passenger seat of his car. To give him a mental break from his mother. Right. His phone's flashlight couldn't help him now.

The light from the store had a faint glow, seemingly more distant than it should have been. Somehow out of reach.

The keys couldn't be far. He dragged his hand against the moist ground. The texture seemed off. What should have been gravel felt sticky, like strands of a web clinging to him.

Ryan heard the rustling and froze.

Must be a bird or something. Had to be. Except that Ryan knew the sound was no bird.

It creaked like old bones, scratched like fingernails against the metal. Ryan raised his gaze, helplessly drawn to the source of it, and was met with shadows.

Darkness moving in the darkness.

The hairs raised on his arms and the back of his neck.

The pitch blackness was a void, tugging at him. Drawing him in, digging into his muscles and twisting around his wrist like manacles. But not empty.

There was something there.

Dropping his groceries, hearing the pasta jar smash, Ryan turned to run, only to stumble over a concrete parking block. He landed hard. Immediately he pushed himself to his feet. The earth clung to his hands, the asphalt clutching like the web of an enormous spider.

Slowly—too slowly—Ryan pulled his hands up and away as bits of his skin tore.

Behind him, the still air rustled in a pattern of breaths. Footsteps echoed across the dark and quiet. Too large and too close.

Ryan turned and craned his neck.

The darkness blinked at him. Features bubbled within the shadows, in and out of focus. Eyes, too many of them, watched him. Ryan felt the heat of that gaze sink into his bones.

"Come on," Ryan whispered, coaxing to life a flicker of flame. He drenched the magic up from the pit of denial he had buried it under. The flames, blue and effervescent, clicked into place. For the first time in years, since Ryan had told himself he was being childish—that he needed to focus on responsibilities, first college and then work—flames sprouted from his fingertips. Warm and swirling with power.

Ryan lifted the flames like a shield.

Only to illuminate the monster.

Ryan couldn't help it—he screamed. As he parted his lips, the creature thrust spider-thin limbs inside of his mouth and wrenched open his jaw—far wider than it could possibly open.

Ryan's scream choked off, blocked, as the arms of the creature jammed down his throat. His head tipped back with the full weight of it as more of the monster crammed its way in. Filling his mouth, the taste of ash and shadow pressed hard against his tongue as tendrils slid down his throat. Piercing deep. Winding. Twisting through his body all the way to his limbs.

Though his brain was half numb with horror, Ryan spotted light in the gloom—his phone lighting up with a message that he'd never get to read.

No. *Sonia.*

He'd never marry her. Never would get the chance. Heirloom ring or otherwise. She'd never find out what happened to him.

Why? Why him?

He'd never done—

The tendrils of shadows pierced his brain, and Ryan thought no more.

THE THING that was like Ryan—but not Ryan—reached down and found both keys and shopping bags easily in the dark.

It paused.

The broken jar reassembled with a jangly pop.

It settled into the car and drove to Ryan's home.

CHAPTER 2

The words of the prophecy swirled through Jun Bear's mind in a dizzying rush. *Protect the magician. Others come to kill her in three months.*

How much time was left?

Jun swallowed before she flipped over the Excel spreadsheet with the date written prominently in the upper corner. July 27, 2012. Two weeks left. If that.

A chill slid down her spine. She'd thought she had more time. She had avoided it. Which was surprisingly easy to do, after she had changed the display on her phone to not show the date and taken down all the calendars in her home. But her Excel sheet automatically generated the date at the top. Usually, she'd fold it over without looking at it.

Thinking about it made things too real. Made it too hard to focus. To get through her day-to-day life. It wasn't like she had the time to obsess over her own mortality every moment—she had a business to run.

Ignoring her problems didn't help. They were out of sight. Just below the surface, always itching for her attention. Waiting for just this quiet moment.

Killers were coming after her.

She went cold as her insides clenched tight and her stomach dropped.

Jun rubbed her arms, trying and failing to coax some warmth into them. She just needed to calm down. Force herself to take some deep breaths. Figure out a plan somehow.

From her roof came a thump that sounded suspiciously like an assassin jumping from the sturdiest branch of her peach tree to the top of her house. The first time she'd heard it was terrifying. This was the second time this week.

Perfect timing. She needed a distraction.

She slipped out the kitchen door to her overgrown back-yard. It was a cold night. The full moon was half-hidden behind the clouds and cast long shadows across her yard. Jun frowned, peering across the gloom.

"Nikolai?" she called out.

Perhaps he wasn't even there. Maybe it was her killer after all, come to finish her off in the quiet of the night.

For a moment, nothing but silence answered her. Then, as if out of the darkness itself, a figure emerged, stepping to the edge of her roof. Just visible in the dim light.

He looked lethal.

His eyes were fierce and pale like the glint of light off a blade's edge. Jawline square, though marred by faint scars. Heavily muscled, with a broad chest. His fingers were agile and capable of throwing his hidden knives within seconds.

He was handsome in the way that a jaguar was; it didn't matter if he was in the jungle or caged. Nothing diminished the power rippling just below the surface. Tonight, Nikolai looked like he was out for blood.

Jun scrutinized the stubborn set of his jaw. "Nikolai, you can't spend the night on my roof again."

He made no reply, not looking away from her. Still and brooding. He seemed about as movable as a statue.

"Come inside." She cut off his argument before he got a chance to say it. "I'll make you a hot chocolate." Jun turned, leaving the door ajar behind her. She didn't bother to check to see if he would follow. Nikolai wouldn't turn down chocolate of any kind.

Jun crossed the kitchen to the stove that was twice as old as she was. She took the kettle and set it to fill under the faucet. As she reached for the jar filled with cocoa powder, she paused at the apron hanging from the oven handle, running her fingers across the cotton pattern of a cartoon trout. Her father's favorite fish. Jun's lip quivered as she pushed away the memory of the last time she'd seen him wear that apron—she'd had no idea that the waffles made that weekend would be the last. She stood just two feet away from where he was murdered. By the same sort of assassins who were after her.

Jun's vision blurred.

She had done such a great job not thinking about it all. Holding strong. She couldn't fall apart. Not now. Not in front of the guy that she...

Jun squeezed her eyes shut, willing herself not to cry.

She tuned out the sound of footsteps behind her that hastened over to the sink, the creak of the turning faucet. The trickle as water poured out of the overflowing kettle. Heavy footsteps crossing the kitchen and stopping in front of her.

One rough finger stroked the underside of her chin, coaxing her to tilt her head up and look into his eyes. Nikolai had worry lines wrinkled into the middle of his forehead as he stared down at her in concern.

"Are you okay?"

"Yeah," Jun said, too quickly. She propped the apron back up on the oven handle without meeting his gaze. She crossed the kitchen, cursing as she poured excess water out of the kettle and set it on heat.

His hand stopped her, settling over hers as she fumbled over the hot cocoa jar, struggling to unlatch the mason jar lid.

"It's okay if you aren't okay." His gaze was heated and locked on her. "I'll help you."

Nikolai had been an ever-present shadow since he'd opened the fortune cookie that had announced killers were after her. Though he'd only let his presence be known occasionally, as he scared off anyone he'd deemed threatening, Jun knew he'd kept close.

"Why..." Jun's voice trailed off.

Why follow her? Why swear to protect her? Why worry about her safety to the point where he'd sleep on her roof?

"You know why." His gaze dropped to her mouth and Jun could feel the heat of it.

Jun bit her lip as she leaned closer, chasing that feeling of strength, that solid reassuring coiled muscle at the heart of Nikolai that would tear apart anything threatening to hurt her.

As Jun pressed closer, Nikolai closed the distance between them with a kiss. He kissed her like he was burning for her. Like he was starving, and she was ambrosia.

He slid his arm around her, pressing Jun closer, as her heart raced. She gasped at the warmth of his touch.

Nikolai backed her against the kitchen wall. His lips left hers as he left a trail of open-mouthed kisses down her neck. She wanted him closer. Welcomed the press of his body against her own. Perhaps she was burning for him too.

He stopped, resting his forehead against her own.

"I'm not going to let anything happen to you." His voice was low with a promise of violence in it. "Anyone who wants to hurt you has to get through me."

CHAPTER 3

On a sleepy road in downtown Hayward was a neat row of indie retail stores and restaurants. The sidewalks were clear. Occasionally a car would drive down the road.

Sitting on a rooftop directly across a newly opened craft store was an assassin—a retired assassin.

Nikolai had a lawn chair set up. He propped his legs against the parapet railing and leaned back with a bag of chips.

Jun's store was quiet. He was making sure of that.

Nikolai leaned in, dropping his chips. He tracked the movements of the woman who was walking down the boulevard as she turned the corner. So far, she was across the street from Jun, simply talking on the phone. Not a threat.

He had just been about to reach down and pick up his Doritos when the woman jaywalked across the street. Heading directly to Jun's craft store.

Nikolai walked across the length of the roof to the fire escape. He took the stairs in huge jumps, landing neatly on the sidewalk below. Jamming his hands into his pockets, he strolled toward the woman.

Mid-thirties. Business attire, walking while scrolling on her phone. Her clothing was professional, though not expensive. She could be on her lunch break or something. It was the sort of outfit that screamed, *Why aren't you at work right now?*

Who goes shopping in a suit?

Maybe someone controlled by strange magic. Magic that tore through their psyche and reason. Magic that took over their senses and directed them toward their target. Magic that hid dormant, insidious, below the surface. Undetected for years, until the moment it rose to the occasion. Snapping free to take over. Magic that could too quickly become lethal.

If a killer could come in any disguise, why not some unassuming professional woman walking down the street? Jun would never see it coming. Not that she paid any attention to any matters involving her own safety.

Nikolai gradually increased his pace until he was just a few steps behind the woman in the business suit. Unnoticed.

"That's the thing, I can't tell what she was thinking—her head was down taking notes the whole time. Yeah, it went exactly like we practiced. I used all the right buzzwords. I even referenced that new study by Marzano." The woman pressed her phone's receiver against her ear, nodding. "I don't know, I messed up somehow. Maybe I should have asked more questions when they asked me if I... Hold on, I'll call you back. I just got to the store. Need to pick up something for Christina's birthday."

The woman paused, her hand on the door to Get Crafty. Nikolai slid his foot, scraping it hard against the ground, and the woman's eyes snapped up; she really hadn't noticed him.

Nikolai glared at her, tense and ready. Waiting for the moment her brown eyes would cloud over black. For her mouth to open wide, revealing the creature that had taken over.

Instead, the woman backed up a couple steps, clutching her phone into a death grip, before powerwalking away from him. She scurried down the street, stopping twice to watch him over her shoulder.

Probably not Jun's potential killer, then.

All right. That was taken care of.

Nikolai scanned the length of the block, checking that it was clear. He caught a quick glimpse of Jun. Her slim frame was crouched over some paperwork. She wore her chunky knitted hat over sleek black hair. Dainty features and dark eyes under long lashes.

Beautiful.

Beautiful and pissed at him.

Nikolai stepped out of view, darting another quick look at her.

Good. She hadn't seen him—she'd told him off the last time she noticed that he was prowling around her store.

Nikolai turned around, heading back up to the roof.

Twenty minutes later, he got the call—it was the ringtone he used to wait for when things got too quiet. One he hadn't heard in months.

"Nikolai speaking."

"Hello, Nikolai." It was the smooth voice of the man Nikolai had known his entire life as the operator. "We've been getting reports about possible magic users in your area. Multiple reports. I've got a team out, but they haven't found the source of it. We could use a veteran, like you."

"I'm still retired." Nikolai narrowed his eyes at the ostentatious gilded display of Jun's store. He was fairly certain that she was keeping under the radar. The prophecy about killers coming after her was threatening enough to keep Jun on her best behavior.

Killers after a magician? Nothing made more sense than for the prophecy to be directed at the assassins from the Order of Saint Christopher. Assassins trained to kill magic users.

After all, he'd been sent to investigate her. Had been on track to eliminate her himself before everything changed.

If one assassin had gotten on her trail, nothing made more sense than for there to be another.

"Things are getting ugly out there. Not sure what it is exactly, but it looks like it's big."

"The Big One?" Nikolai scoffed.

The hunters of the Order talked rumors about the Big One for generations. Rumor had it that magicians of old, like Merlin, were more than myth. That there were magicians capable of power beyond the pale. Powers that went beyond the ability to damage others. Powers that could threaten the very shape of reality.

A magician just like Jun.

Like fuck he was going to let them know about her.

Would it make sense though to get closer to the Order? Take on another couple of hits. Track down a few other magicians. Make sure to keep the target off Jun's back?

Which would mean keeping Jun defenseless while he was off hunting some low-life gangsters. With not even a week and a half left until killers were supposed to descend upon her and take her from him.

Yeah, right.

"Can't be sure. More likely it's multiple magic users working together. We're hearing rumors of a coven."

"Never heard of that before." The magicians he'd seen—prior to Jun, of course—were bloodthirsty, stone-cold killers. Mindless serial killers, the lot of them. Not at all capable of working together.

"What kind of reports?"

"Unexplained power outages, some missing persons. Odd nine-one-one calls. Got one about an abduction in a grocery store parking lot. By the time the police came, nothing came of it. False alarms. On their own, nothing to worry about. But the frequency of the calls is suspicious. It's not normal for the activity to be cropping up like this. We've had to pull in extra teams from other jurisdictions."

"Damn," Nikolai muttered under his breath. That complicated things. Jun would be veiled by whatever other magic user was out there. But the last thing she needed was more effective hunters out there on her trail.

The thought crept in, worry whispering in the back of his mind. What if it wasn't the assassins who were behind this? Concentrated magic activity? What if this was something else entirely?

"Haven't seen anything," Nikolai lied. "I'll let you know if I do."

Before Jun, he wouldn't have entertained the thought that witches were cognizant enough to team up. Help one another.

He'd been wrong about Jun.

He was beginning to get an insight into how little he'd truly known about magic all along.

"Well, let me know if you're interested."

"Yeah."

Nikolai hung up. It wasn't ever going to happen.

CHAPTER 4

Victoria heard it. Like a whisper on the edge of her awareness, tugging at her. Or a frequency just out of range of human hearing. Jangling. Vibrating in the air. Calling to her. It wasn't a true sound—at least the others didn't seem to be reacting to it.

"All right, all right," Victoria muttered to herself.

Obviously, the spirits had something to say to her.

She pulled out her headphones and Shakira's "She Wolf" fell away. She couldn't have her music drown out the world right now.

Immediately, she was bombarded by the sounds of the party. The stereo was pumping with that new Swedish House Mafia single, "Don't You Worry Child."

Spirits were high. Xochitl had hacked into the radio waves for the Order. They hadn't been sniffing around coven members as frequently, and now everyone knew why. Nikolai Visiliev, the most lethal assassin to come out of the Order in decades, had officially retired a few weeks ago. No one knew why. Xochitl had even broken into his paperwork. As far as the report went, his physicals and psych evaluations were all normal. Seemed that he just up and quit after his last assignment went sour. Apparently, they got their man, but his whole team went down.

Strange that he'd let the death of his team stop him now. It wasn't like this was the first time he'd lost team members. Ruthless, efficient, and for the past five years, Visiliev had been assigned to the West Coast. Their territory. Victoria had assumed that he'd go on hunting their coven and their kind forever.

Visiliev was the asshole who had taken out Samuel's little brother. Samuel hadn't even noticed that his kid brother was on the Order's radar when Nikolai swept in. The kid was barely a teenager.

Now, the Order was scrambling to replace that workaholic murderer.

It was a good time to be a witch in the Greater Northern Pacific Coven. No more constantly looking over their shoulders. No more consulting with destiny cards and star charts when you wanted to go off on a three-day vacation. Things were finally looking up.

Members of her coven mingled and flirted. Red solo cups were filled to the brim with spiked punch and sangria. Jones had spilled half a cup on one of Samuel's cracked leather sofas.

Samuel Brown, their fearless leader and head warlock, was wearing a witch hat. One from the discount bin at party city, made entirely out of polyester. It kept falling over his eyes as he went around the living room taking people's topping requests.

Still, the words whispered to Victoria. Cutting through the sounds of the party. Like a foreign language swirling around her mind, demanding her attention.

Their most pressing threat had been eliminated, but the whispers remained. What did fate want now?

"Pizza should be here in fifteen minutes, people."

"Did you get the deluxe veggie?"

"No, we're not ordering from Feelin' Saucy. Their new delivery girl brought over *cold* pizza."

"Come on, man. That's the good stuff. It's worth the wait."

"I am too old for cold pizza. I deserve better things in life."

Victoria shook her head, tuning out the conversation. Focusing, she drowned out everything but the soft velvet of her messenger bag. She slipped her hands inside and pulled out her cards.

The tarot cards were stiff and solid. Dependable. Victoria shuffled the cards, feeling the power of them warm through her fingers. Heat raced up her arms and the back of her neck.

All her attention funneled down to the cards in her hands as she wove them in a familiar pattern. Not so much shuffling them as she was allowing the cards the freedom to rearrange themselves, to present the necessary images and reveal all of the hidden truths in brutally plain images.

Taking a deep breath, Victoria stilled her mind, addressing the persistent whisper. Reaching. Calling her.

She focused on her question, letting it crystalize. Until she could touch each letter of each word. The question in her mind shifted into a solid presence as she shuffled through her cards, breaking the deck into three, then putting all her cards back together.

What do I need to know?

The sound of the party faded to nothing. There was no sound but that of her own inhales as she drew the first card from her deck, placing it down on Samuel's Ikea coffee table.

The first card of her draw landed heavily, with the weight of more than simple cardstock.

Victoria flipped the card over, revealing the Devil.

She gasped without meaning to. Taking in the smiling, almost lude expression on his horned face. The chains in his hands, holding on to a human couple.

So you are behind this. Victoria's thoughts drifted to Nikolai, his powerful build and all the angry scars running in patterns along his face and arms.

She'd seen him up close and personal once. Victoria had gone to the campus library, checking out a source, and there he was. Victoria had immediately looked the other way, summoning up light magic for illusion and misdirection. She'd hurried away from him as quickly as she could.

She'd had to put up with her Give for a month. In her case it wasn't the worst thing in the world—an unquench-able desire for fudge chocolate. For the first week, the siren call of chocolate was irresistible and she'd gained seven pounds. But it was worth it. She'd gotten away alive.

Nikolai hadn't been there for her. He'd targeted some other hapless victim. No one that Victoria knew. Not that she could do much to help anyone who was already on Visiliev's radar. He was a notoriously fast-acting assassin.

Victoria looked back on the face of the Devil—the one who was working behind the scenes. She had a sense that this devil was pulling all the strings. Had a hold on some-thing that was to come.

That was bad.

With a sinking feeling, Victoria looked at that inhuman grin and thought to herself that perhaps this had nothing to do with Visiliev. This was something else entirely.

What do you need me to know?

Victoria drew the second card from the top of the deck. Felt the rightness of it in her hand as she turned it over on the table.

Revealing the Tower.

Victoria stilled.

It wasn't a card she'd drawn often.

Her eyes traced over the lightning strike and the burning windows. The horrified bodies tumbling out, falling to the ground below.

This means that something is coming.

Chaos was on its way. Chaos and destruction.

One thing that was clear was that things were about to change.

But what would this change lead to? What did all this mean?

Victoria pulled the last card from the top of the deck. The card to reveal what all of this would result in.

The paper heated her fingertips, burning her before she flipped it over to reveal the image that lay beneath. What was at stake here? What were all these signs pointing to?

Death. The last card she pulled was the Death card.

Victoria's vision zeroed in on the eyeless socket. The skull of the knight staring out blankly back at her.

Her fingertips burned where they touched the cards. Her vision blacked out.

The party was gone.

Her coven was gone.

Victoria was in a field. In the dark. Alone.

All she could hear were her own gasping breaths.

What was going on?

Victoria turned around. She'd had visions before, but this felt like no vision.

She could feel the harsh wind on her back, the grass and stiff weeds cutting into the sides of her feet exposed by her sandals. Victoria breathed out a shaky breath, which came out as a visible fog in the cold.

She had no memory of this empty field, filled with weeds.

Then Victoria heard the cry for help.

She wrapped her jacket around herself, rushing to the north, in the direction of the screams. As she ran toward it, a group of people, teenagers in hoodies and jeans, ran past her. Terror written on their expressions. They jostled her, their shoulders bumping into hers as they ran past.

"What's..." Victoria tried asking them, but they did not stop to speak. Just running blindly away.

That's when she felt the field start to shake. A step that rattled the whole world, like an earthquake in miniature.

More screams though now the sound was distorted, hanging up high in the air.

Victoria looked up and faced the eyes of a giant skull. Darkness lingered in those empty sockets—a void too deep for her to see through.

A giant skeleton. Easily over thirty feet tall. Its hands were bony grasping claws. Clenched within skeletal fingers, a figure twisted and screamed, frantically trying to get away.

The creature growled, the sound reverberating like a motor slowed down. Each thud of its non-beating heart thudded against the air with violence.

The creature of bone and death lifted the screaming figure to its mouth, opening its jaw wide. The screams rose to an even higher pitch, desperate, before they were abruptly broken off with a sickening crunch.

Victoria heard the swoosh and thunk of something heavy falling to the ground. A ball of hair that turned, revealing a face twisted in pain. The rest of the decapitated body the creature tipped over, letting streams of red rush down to its mouth. Blood trails dripped down the open jaw, staining the bones of its neck a garish red.

The giant skeleton let the rest of the body slip back down, falling to the earth in a thud.

The creature zeroed its attention on Victoria instead. Those blank eyes were riveted toward her, and the skull lifted its jaw into a lipless grin as it reached the bony fingers down for her.

Frozen, Victoria stood rooted to the ground as the jagged fingers of the creature wrapped around her body. Cold bone pinched against her, immobilizing her. Victoria was numb as her body was lifted into the air.

What was happening?

No. It was just a vision. This had to just be a vision.

No. She was back at Samuel's house. She had pulled up a tarot card.

What was happening? This was a vision. She was trapped in a vision. But it was too real. Too real. Those bony fingers weren't going away. She was still getting pulled up into the air. Closer and closer to the creature's face. To the jaws that were opened wide.

All around her were loud, desperate screams, coming out of her raw throat.

"Victoria!"

All she could see were those sightless eyes burned into the front of her vision.

"Victoria!" She felt hands on her shoulder, grasping her, concerned She pushed them away, desperate. How had this happened? How could she have gotten herself into this? Why didn't she pull away? How did she end up getting trapped like this? She couldn't let it end like this. This wasn't her end. This wasn't how she died. She wasn't supposed to die. She was at Samuel's house, at a party. They were about to get pizza.

The hands on her shoulders were warm. Worried.

All she could feel was cold bone, pinching her. Crushing the life out of her.

"Someone take a look at her spread. She did a reading."

"Devil, Tower and Death—those are major arcana cards."

The voices billowing out of the skull's mouth—why were they so familiar?

As the skull spoke, Victoria tried to scramble away from the movements of its jaw. Her entire field of vision was taken up with teeth. Rotten and crumbling. Close enough to see bits of skin and torn flesh wedged in the crevices. And the darkness beyond, as the creature opened its mouth wide.

Then it was gone.

"Victoria! Jesus, what is it? What do you see?" It was Samuel. He was staring down at her with wide, worried eyes. His stupid witch hat had fallen off.

Victoria gasped, blinking rapidly. She leapt up, wrapping her arms around Samuel. With her heart racing painfully fast, she clung to Samuel's solid presence. Her eyes filled with tears. She couldn't stop shaking.

He wrapped his hands around her, patting her back awkwardly.

The field was gone. The darkness was gone. She was back in Samuel's living room. Surrounded by red solo cups and the concerned gazes of her entire coven. Staring at her. As she struggled not to cry.

"Victoria, think."

She took a deep, shuddering breath. Had to warn them.

"The cards called me, and I was answering the call."

Victoria ground her knuckle into her brow as if she could push away the image of what she'd seen. "Asking what I needed to know."

"What does this mean?" Samuel was pointing to the Tower. Then to the skeleton in armor.

"Chaos and death. It's coming."

Samuel pointed to the Devil card. "Who is this? Is this Visiliev? Is he coming back?"

She thought back to the whispers. How they had called to her. Warning her.

Victoria shook her head. When she closed her eyes, her vision was filled with the gaze of that giant monster.

Chaos and death on a grand scale.

"It was more like the end of the world."

CHAPTER 5

The storefront was small, with rather large windows emblazoned with the phrase 'Get Crafty' in golden trim. Rows of pastel yarn lined the display in all varieties—merino, alpaca, cashmere and silk. Colorful swaths of floral fabrics, crocheted figures and stationary supplies rounded out the display. A banner affixed to the glass with packing tape read 'Grand Opening, 20% Off Storewide.'

Behind the cash register, Jun sat on a stool and knitted without looking down, with long practiced familiarity. She glanced over an Excel spreadsheet with marketing expenses, frowning. She finished a row and stuck her knitting needles into a fluffy yarn ball.

Still empty. It was a rainy Tuesday, mid-day. It wasn't like she expected a huge crowd. But it would have been nice to have at least one customer.

Closing the binder with a snap, Jun dropped the documents into a drawer and pulled out a bowl of dry cereal. She tossed a handful into her mouth.

The drawer rustled with the scrit-scrit of little paws. Jun

opened it back up and a little white rabbit appeared, as if out of nowhere.

"Hey, there." Jun smiled.

The little fellow approached her cereal bowl, holding out a paw. Jun scooped up some pieces and handed them over.

The white rabbit—that was not a rabbit—munched the cereal cheerfully.

Jun sighed and scratched the rabbit behind the ear, where he liked it. "It's only the first week. Business is sure to pick up."

The white rabbit turned around and regarded Jun solemnly, nodding.

Jun perked up as two older ladies holding large coffee cups pointed at the store and paused in their walk.

The two ladies stepped into her store, and Jun nodded to them in greeting.

"Good morning," Jun said as the rabbit jumped on the top of her head.

The ladies showed no sign that they thought it odd that the shopkeeper sat at the cash register with a rabbit perched on her knitted purple hat. Then again, no one ever saw the little guy if she didn't point him out.

Jun focused very hard on not looking at her first customers of the day, holding her breath as they perused the stationary.

"Your granddaughter would love that." The woman with dangly earrings held up an eraser shaped like a kitten in a box.

"Adorable," her friend with curls and turquoise eyeshadow agreed. "They come up with the cutest new things. Wish they had made this when we were kids."

The door-chimes rang again, and in walked Nikolai. He

narrowed his pale eyes at the pair of ladies, glaring at them as if he had learned that they were personally responsible for the rising cost of gas, or like they drowned kittens in their spare time. Heavily muscled, with scars and burn marks running down his arms, he looked like a beast.

Wait.

How did he get here so fast? This was way too fast to be a coincidence.

How did he always manage to get to her store within a minute of a customer? It was impossibly fast. Unless...

Was he stalking the people who came to her store?

Jun refrained from rolling her eyes at him, and from grabbing her nearest yarn ball and chucking it at his big glaring head.

The women whispered to one another, eyes darting to him. Ms. Dangly-Earrings returned the eraser and the two of them walked out of the store, giving the newcomer a wide berth.

When the glass door shut and the two ladies had walked off in a hurry, Jun drummed her fingers against the counter. Enough was enough. It was time to say something.

"Nikolai," she called out in her overly polite business voice.

His jaw clenched stubbornly before he looked back at her. "Yeah?"

"I made graphs predicting the number of customers and the expected range of profit I'd likely have in this area. But I've gotten close to no sales."

"That's too bad." He didn't look surprised.

"It's too low to be a random chance. Either I've made some gross errors in my plans... or you've been actively scaring all my customers away." Jun watched him to gauge his reaction.

Nikolai stared hard at her back wall, tense and not saying a word. His silence was damning.

She sighed. "Stop scaring away my customers, Nikolai."

"Sorry," he said. Though the expression on his face was not at all apologetic.

"Seriously, did you think that those two little old ladies were trying to kill me?" Jun opened the drawer back up and grabbed her cereal bowl. Scooping up a handful, she paused to pass a piece up to the white rabbit before stress eating.

"The prophecy said three months." Nikolai scowled. "In case you've forgotten. It said that someone is coming to kill you in three months. That's in less than a week."

Jun sighed and pushed her cereal away, appetite soured. She plucked the rabbit off her hat, placing him in front of the bowl, letting him have at it.

Nikolai had been like this for months. Tense. Scowling at every shadow, grimacing at every corner as if her murderer were lurking in wait. Ever since he had read the prophecy in that fortune cookie telling him to *protect the magician.*

It was enough to make Jun want to find another fortune cookie and smash it in retaliation. But she knew better than to ignore the prophecies. Last time she'd done that, it had resulted in a magnitude 6.5 earthquake and a team of assassins out for her blood.

"You think those grandmas are the killers?" Jun held her hand on her hip, raising her eyebrows.

"If I could use magic, I would definitely choose a form you weren't expecting. I'd change my appearance to look harmless so your guard would be down."

"That's only if the people who are after me are magicians. They could be assassins like you."

Nikolai pinched the bridge of his nose and took a deep

breath. "Not if you lay low. If you can manage that, there won't be any reason for any more teams of assassins to come after you."

"So you've said," Jun said. "Every single day since you read the fortune. I get it. No big magic feats."

Nikolai sighed and took Jun's hand. He looked seriously into her eyes as he held her palm in his much larger hands. "Just until this three-month thing is over. You promised to at least try."

Jun huffed, dodging that haunted look in his eyes as she muttered about overprotective assassins who needed a hobby.

"Keeping you alive is like a full-time job. You'd think that you'd help me out a bit." Nikolai traced his fingers along her knuckles, his pale gaze intense.

It wasn't that Jun didn't want to take this seriously. But it wasn't like she could think about her own mortality every moment of every day. Living every moment wondering what kind of mistake she'd make that would be her last just didn't feel like living. Besides, she had a business to run.

But she had to throw the guy a bone. All the stress was going to give him a heart attack. Holding his gaze, Jun nodded reluctantly.

Nikolai let out a breath he was holding, and tension eased in his shoulders.

"But you have to promise me that you are going to stop scaring my customers away."

Nikolai looked up sharply, mouth opened and ready to argue with her.

"Look," Jun cut him off. "I get that you're trying to protect me. I appreciate that. But you weren't the only one to get a prophecy that day. I was right next to you, opening mine, and it told me to build this store. I have to be here. I have to do this."

Nikolai looked like he'd swallowed a lemon dipped in hot sauce.

"Jun, it's too risky." He shook his head. "I don't want to scare you, but I don't think you know how brutal it can be. I've seen too many people killed by magicians. Getting killed by magic is probably the most horrific way to go."

He looked away from her, clenching his jaw tight.

What was he thinking about? Was he remembering all those people killed by magic?

Was he imagining her instead, replacing those countless victims?

Or was he realizing that Jun herself was a magician. That Jun was capable of killing people in all the same gruesome ways he'd seen.

That she wasn't just some girl that he thought was pretty... She was a magician, and he was a magician-killer.

Yes, the two of them shared a few kisses, but how could they ever become something more?

They were supposed to be enemies.

He was going to realize that he was making a mistake. She waited for the other shoe to drop, for the moment Nikolai came to the conclusion that he didn't belong here, pushing himself to the limit just to guard someone like *her*.

"I just want you to be safe." He leaned in, closer to her. Tracing a line against her cheek as he stared at her mouth. His touch was warm.

Jun shivered, heart racing.

He slid a finger against her lower lip, in a light touch like he couldn't help himself. Like it wasn't in his power to move away from her. Like he was helplessly drawn to her. "Let me save you."

"I know that what I'm asking for doesn't make sense. But we're dealing with killers and fate. There might not be anything either of us can do about it."

Nikolai's eyes flashed in anger. He looked ready to keep arguing with her.

Jun took his hand and smoothed her palm against his. The tips of her fingers ghosted over his callouses. "If this is all the time I've got left, I want to live it. I want a chance to run my own business. It's important to me."

"Fine." He spat out the word like it was choking him. "I'll stop scaring away your customers."

Jun smiled at him.

"But I'm staying at the store," he added.

"Wait. What?"

"Actually, this works out. There's no chance that anyone could slip past me if I'm already here."

"Absolutely not. You cannot threaten everyone that comes in."

"What am I supposed to do then, watch them attack you?" Nikolai glared at her.

"Well, obviously you can kill my killers," Jun muttered, spelling it out for him. "But only if you're sure they're killers."

Nikolai ran his fingers through his hair, and Jun was sure that he was going to keep arguing with her. She'd heard it all before. Jun braced herself for a fight.

His eyes locked on hers as Nikolai studied her expression. After a moment he nodded.

Jun's front bell chimes jangled and for once she ignored it, lost in his gaze.

Nikolai was close enough that she could feel the ghost of his breath across her lips. His gaze flicked to the side as her entrance chimes went off. Suddenly Nikolai stiffened and turned away, staring hard at whoever it was that came through her door.

"Jun, isn't that..." Nikolai trailed off as he stared at the customer.

Frowning, Jun craned her head to get a look. She froze, wide-eyed. She felt like the baby who got the candy taken away as she recognized the face she thought she'd never see again.

Suzie Albrecht. Suzie, with her perfectly curled blonde hair and manicured fingers. Jun's old college roommate. Suzie, who hated Jun. Hated her with an unprovoked and undisguised loathing. *What is she doing here?*

Jun hadn't seen Suzie since she'd graduated, and that was months ago.

Though they'd lived together for a little over a year, and though Jun still had her number saved somewhere (probably), they hadn't spoken. There was no reason for the two of them to speak.

They definitely weren't friends.

They had nothing in common.

They lived completely different lives. Suzie had bragged about landing some fancy tech internship that she was going to start after graduation. The two of them never even officially said goodbye. Jun just returned to the dorm to see that Suzie had managed to pack up and move out before her. She'd thought that was the end of that. Or at least it was supposed to be.

Maybe Suzie being here was just a coincidence?

How could it be a coincidence?

Suzie was loitering around her store. Just walking through her stationary aisle, running a perfectly rounded nail over Jun's novelty erasers.

Jun forced herself to look away, mouthing to Nikolai, "What is she doing here?"

He shrugged as he tracked Suzie, bringing his arms to his sides.

Suzie drifted through the aisles almost aimlessly. Looking at the displays that Jun had set up by researching color theory and agonized over.

"This is so weird," Jun muttered to Nikolai.

"Why?" he asked without taking his eyes off the ex-roommate.

"Suzie never showed any interest in this kind of stuff before. She called it dumb." Jun couldn't take her eyes off of Suzie, weighing two different yarn balls in her hand. The turquoise ball was merino wool, while the periwinkle was a chenille yarn. In college, Jun had knitted both types in their dorm while Suzie muttered that she wouldn't be caught dead playing with string. Suzie replaced them both on the shelves, strolling along the aisles.

Jun leaned to watch her in the round security mirror.

Suzie's reflection walked stiffly, surrounded by hand-crafted notebooks. Pointing at paper crafts and paintbrushes like she was conducting an orchestra. Her manicured fingers stopped at the polymer clay display. Jun had molded display animals. A fluffy chinchilla eating a giant sunflower seed. A miniature burger and an ice cream cone. She even crafted tiny rabbits. A white rabbit bursting out of a top hat. Jun had also made a black rabbit holding a mug of tea with two paws.

Suzie reached for the display, her fingers hovering near the clay animals, and then reached past it. She grabbed one of the larger polymer clay kits.

Business-like, Suzie walked back to the front of the store.

If she thought Jun's gigantic bodyguard was strange, she

showed no signs of it. Instead, Suzie placed the kit in front of the cash register and looked up at Jun expectantly.

Just welcome her to the store. Be casual. Tell her there's a sale.

Don't say anything stupid. Don't say anything stupid. DON'T say anything STUPID.

Jun's eyes dropped to the clay kit. "Hiya, ex-roomie." Her voice turned high-pitched. "Thought you hated me and never wanted to see me again." *Damn it.*

Suzie watched Jun blankly. Not even dignifying Jun's greeting with a response.

Jun gulped, took in a deep breath, and muttered, "That'll be thirty-four dollars and twenty-nine cents. Twenty percent off."

Suzie reached into her alligator skin clutch, pulling out a matching wallet. She fished out two twenties.

The light overhead flickered and failed in the time it took Jun to blink. Casting Suzie's face in shadows that transformed her. In the dark, those lovely pink cheeks were stripped away, revealing bone underneath. Suzie's pretty, haughty face was a mask painted over a skeletal void.

The moment passed, and the room was fully lit, with no one commenting on the change. It happened so fast, could Nikolai have just missed it?

Did that really happen?

Jun bit her lip. It didn't feel real. Like she had just imagined the whole thing.

Should she say something to Nikolai?

When it was probably anxiety or stress playing tricks on her.

Was she really going to have him chase after shadows that were more likely just figments of her imagination?

Jun ducked down, opening the register, mentally calculating her change. Rooting through the cash drawer for the least crumpled bills and shiniest coins.

When Jun looked back up, Suzie had already walked halfway out the store, clutching the clay.

"Hey! You forgot your change." Jun stared at the bills helplessly, wondering if Suzie meant this as some kind of insult. Like Jun was a charity case. "Do you at least want your receipt?"

Jun groaned when Suzie was out of the store. "Why does she make me feel so dumb?"

"What I'd like to know is why you are more terrified of your old roommate than the literal killers coming after you." Nikolai said it like it was a joke, but his jaw tensed as he looked away.

Jun bit her tongue. She wanted to write it off. To say a blithe comment that death is easier than social awkwardness. But death was too close to be funny.

The worst part was how permanent it was. Jun swallowed, pushing down the thought of all the times she had tapped out a text to her father, telling him a joke, just to find that the message did not send.

Too close. And death was coming for her.

She didn't want to think about it. She didn't want to think about any of it.

Jun pulled Nikolai closer. He leaned in as she tugged his arm, though she could never hope to move his bulk on her own. Grabbing a bit of life, that spark of connection between them a little bit closer.

Until they were almost nose to nose.

Close enough to feel the heat in his gaze. A heat that echoed through her, dancing across her skin and lighting up her senses. Until she was hyperaware of his sharp inhale. Of his lips parting. The way his eyes dilated, taking all of her in.

He was an assassin. He'd killed people like her. Had been sent after her specifically. When did he start making her feel safe?

She placed her fingers against that strong jaw until he looked at her.

"What do I have to be afraid of? There's nothing scarier out there than you," she teased, looking at him up through her eyelashes.

Nikolai closed the space between them with a kiss. His lips pressed against hers, burning away her fears. Burning away her questions, her anxiety. Cutting through it all.

She was done feeling afraid.

She had wasted so much time when she could have had this with him for months. Felt alive this entire time.

She could have that. For at least another week. Until her killers came for her.

CHAPTER 6

Ryan smiled as he scooped another spoonful of cake and dropped it into his mouth—double chocolate with pink icing spelling out the 'con' in congratulations. He tasted neither the sugar nor the butter. None of the component parts of flour, egg, or milk registered. Not the chocolate or the sharp sugary crunch of sprinkles. The moist fudge tasted like ash on his tongue.

He was getting hungry.

As he dug his spoon into the slice of the retirement cake again, Ryan scanned the office. Always on the lookout for the next potential meal. Typically, he wouldn't hunt close to an establishment tied to him, but of course it wouldn't hurt to take a look.

Front and center was the wrinkled face of Beatrice. She wore a party hat with "happy retirement" written in Sharpie. All of that experience would be quite rich. She was well seasoned with years that would be textured and smooth. The young tended to be grittier. They hadn't quite ironed out their emotions. Hadn't quite established who they were or who they wanted to be. Of course, Beatrice was off limits.

Every few minutes new coworkers approached her, saying kind words. Some of them even meant them.

Balloons were hastily affixed with blue painter tape onto the ceiling, along with dollar store streamers. There was Justin from accounting. Not yet forty and not yet balding. Only his rectangular pair of bifocal glasses marked the passing of the years. He was too thin with energy that was almost stringy. No. He, like the others here, was a disappointment.

Ryan's gaze flicked to Erin. An intern, younger than the others. She had the high cheekbones and bright eyes that many would describe as quite pretty. As his eyes met hers, Erin blushed and ducked her head.

Interesting.

Attraction and betrayal were lovely flavors.

She'd do.

He waited.

Four minutes later, Erin placed her red solo cup down at her desk and headed over to Beatrice. Off to say her goodbyes to her coworker for the last time.

Ryan licked his spoon clean as he reached into the drawer of his desk. He pulled out a plastic baggie with one small, unmarked pill inside. Pressing the spoon against the pill, Ryan crushed it into a powder. He took a pinch of the stuff on his fingers and walked toward Erin's unattended drink. The powder dissolved into the liquid completely, without a trace. Ryan walked away just as he was hit by another wave of hunger.

It wouldn't be much longer now.

CHAPTER 7

Victoria stared at the card in her hand with enough heat to burn through the cardstock.

"I don't know what this means," she murmured.

What felt like hundreds of times, she'd asked the cards. *What can we do?* Every single draw, she pulled the Star card. It was a symbol of hope, and clearly the answer to what to do about the chaos and destruction to come. The problem was, Victoria had no idea what the Star meant.

None of the draws made any sense to her.

Victoria let out a deep breath, clearing her mind. She pictured the giant skull monster. A bit of research amongst the coven had revealed it to be a Gashadokuro. A monster built out of the rage of bodies that had died in wars. Built out of mass graves, the skeletal giants wander in the darkest hours of the night. Fueled by their hatred against the living, they lived until their bodies burned out, enjoying nothing more than eating humans. Unstoppable. Continuing on until the energy of all that hatred burned out of them and they finally crumbled back into dust.

They were supposed to be rare. They were built from mass graves of spoiling, rotting, forgotten bodies. How did she get a vision of one? Now? In modern times? That kind of thing wasn't meant to be possible anymore. Monsters like that were supposed to be a myth. How was there that much pain and hatred coming that would allow those things to come again?

Victoria sighed as she dropped the card back into the deck. Shuffling. Once more surrendering to the rhythm of the cards, allowing fate to work and flow through her fingers. To show her the truth of all things.

Another simple three card draw. She focused on the question.

How do we stop it? Without meaning to, her vision was filled with the visage of that wide rotting smile. She shuddered without being able to stop herself.

She flipped the first card to reveal the same thing she had drawn over and over again in multiple readings. The Star. A woman kneeling in the water. One foot in the water, the other on land. *Someone who has a foot in both realities, real and magic, perhaps.* The Star card was a blessing. The best thing to see after drawing the Tower. It was hope. *Yes, I get that. But how?*

Victoria placed her finger on the second card, feeling the warmth of it light up the pads of her fingers. She flipped it and laid Strength on the table. Another Major Arcana card. Recently, those were the only kinds she seemed to pull. On the Strength card, a woman leaned over a lion, her face passive as she clasped the lion's jaws.

Now to bring this all together, what does this lead to? Victoria pulled the next card from the deck, the Magician. The first Major Arcana card. The Magician stood in front of his altar. There lay all the tools at his disposal. Sword, magic rod, pentagram, chalice. He had all the resources he needed to succeed.

But what does all of this mean? How does this all fit together?

"Victoria?"

Samuel's greeting jolted her out of her thoughts. She blinked and looked around. She was at his house. Everyone else was gone. At the start of the emergency meeting, she had noticed the others watching her warily. Now she and Samuel were alone. Outside the windows came the yellow glow of streetlamps. Night had fallen.

Samuel smiled tentatively at her. "How's it going?"

Victoria shook her head at her spread. "I keep trying. I've pulled the Star over and over again. Some of the other cards in the spread I've pulled before. I don't know what any of this means."

"You've been at this for hours."

Hours? Really? It felt like she had just started. Though one eye was twitching, and a slight headache bloomed just behind her right eye.

"You didn't see the creature. I need to stop it."

Samuel nodded, pressing his index fingers into his temple. "Well, what's this one?"

"The Star? The Star is hope."

Samuel pointed to the next two. "And then you got Strength and the Magician. Could it be that we just need to find a powerful magician?"

"The cards aren't meant to be read that literally." Victoria leaned back in Samuel's cracked leather sofa, looking up to the ceiling.

Could it really be that simple? Find the strongest magician?

"Why would we need to find a strong magician anyway?"

Samuel held up his fingers, inspecting the blackened

ends—like nail polish, except that the color extended to his fingertips.

"Magic always has a price." Samuel examined the evidence that was written into his skin, how dark magic leached away his life force. Taking an hour, a minute, a day with each use. "But that price is different for everyone. Almost anyone can use powerful magic. Magic is magic; that never changes. Change the cost of it. Think of all you could do if you weren't limited by the cost of your magic. It's said that the most powerful witches and warlocks barely feel the cost. Think of the things you could do. You could rule the world with that kind of raw power."

Victoria had channeled dark magic once and only once. She'd immediately fallen to the ground gasping, her throat raw. Smoke had filled her and she had been drowning in it. Breathless. The weight of all that power was pressure. Constricting her chest. Squeezing her lungs. She had been sure it was going to kill her.

It was her one and only foray into dark magic; the price had been too high.

Dark magic burned right through reality. Powerful. Raw. But each use took something away. Mind or body, it always had a cost.

But the *possibilities.*

Dark magic had opened a window in her mind. She'd watched moments that should have been lost secrets. Clear as if she had been watching them in a movie theater. Saw the truth in what had happened to her. Though she'd only been a child, and her memories were all jumbled and out of order, she'd seen her mother. Seen the twitchy look on her face as she'd carried her—

"Is there any reason why it couldn't mean that?" Samuel tapped just below the Magician card.

She blinked as Samuel's question pulled her out of her memories, and took a deep breath to refocus.

"Well, no. That would be a pretty direct interpretation."

Samuel shrugged. "Maybe the cards are trying to help you out by being direct."

Victoria wiped her palm over her face, wiping away non-existent sweat. If only she could wipe away the feeling of failure, or all those hours she had wasted trying without any luck.

"Hey," Samuel said.

Victoria looked up at him through the fingers obscuring her vision.

"It's not like you caused this. You're only the one who discovered it. Stop blaming yourself. This isn't your fault."

Victoria shook her head. "It's not like that. I need to find the answer. I need to do something about it."

"This isn't all on you." Samuel tapped his index finger against his chin. "Maybe we need to bring out more fire power."

"What do you mean?"

"It's about time that we had a summoning."

CHAPTER 8

Nikolai rearranged the merino wool display for the third time, fairly certain that he was screwing up the color theory technique Jun was going for. *How did I go from an assassin to stacking yarn balls in an Indie craft store?*

He jerked his head in the direction of the high-pitched chime at the entrance. The door chimes at Get Crafty were quickly becoming Nikolai's least favorite sound. Abandoning the project was probably for the best. It wasn't like he was going to be able to make her display look pretty anyway. He was still colorblind.

Nikolai stepped in front of Jun at the cash register. Keeping her out of sight from whoever had entered the store.

Through the front doors of Get Crafty came a very average-looking man. Late twenties to early thirties, tall and scrawny, with a meandering gait. He wore a simple graphic T-shirt. One of the kinds sold at Target. There was nothing threatening about his posture.

Nikolai couldn't say exactly what it was about the man

that put him on edge. Just that there was something off about him.

Even though he was average, painfully average, Nikolai couldn't stop thinking that there was something wrong. Something about the way that the light avoided him. It was as if he was doused in shadow as he walked. As if he was slightly dimmed out, darker than the rest of the world.

Nikolai casually slipped his hands into the inner lining of his sleeves—right where he kept his knives. Tracking the man as he strolled through the store, who now ran his finger down a stack of sketchbooks.

The man's wandering path looped past the register. Close enough to smell his Axe body spray, and underneath it, the metallic whiff of ozone—like burnt chlorine hanging off of him. The smell was old, but unmistakable. Magic.

As he rounded the corner, Nikolai saw it—threads of darkness, so thin that they almost blended into the shadows that leaked out of his body in a web.

This man, whoever he was pretending to be, wasn't fully human.

Not anymore.

Nikolai tensed. He backed into Jun until she was blocked by the bulk of his body. Ignoring how she muttered at him, "You are the absolute worst at being retired."

The man who wasn't a man hummed the jingle of a spearmint gum commercial with his hands in his pockets. Strolling up and down the aisles. He paused in front of the rows of yarn that Nikolai had just rearranged, rolling his fingers between the strands.

After a minute or so, he grabbed some yarn and a pair of knitting needles. As he approached the register, Nikolai pulled out his blade, holding it at his side in a hammer grip, determining the best angle to pierce straight through the man's heart.

Nikolai was poised, aim calculated, ready to attack the moment the man showed the first hint of aggression.

Jun pressed her hand on his shoulder, leaning around him. She stood slightly on her tippy toes. "The periwinkle yarn is five dollars, and the knitting needles are seven sixty-five. If you were interested in a bamboo pair, those are currently on sale for—"

"No, that's fine. I'll get these two."

"All right, I'll just ring you up, then." Jun grabbed the objects from behind Nikolai and scanned them.

The man slid a credit card across the counter, with a casual smile plastered across his face. As Jun looked away, the man locked eyes with Nikolai. His grin grew wider, lips parting, revealing the shadows that dripped down his teeth like fangs.

"Would you like to sign up for our rewards program...?" Jun checked his card for his name. "Ryan?"

"Sure, sounds great." Ryan's lips snapped back to his tight-lipped smile.

Jun typed the man's name into her register as Nikolai clenched his blade in a white-knuckle grip. Glaring at the placid expression on Ryan's face.

"Thank you." Jun handed the card back to the man, somehow oblivious to the tension in the room. "You got three points so far. If you get to fifteen you get fifty percent off, or a free yarn ball."

Ryan nodded, tucking his knitting supplies under his arm. Still pretending that he was nothing more than a customer. That he hadn't let the mask slip for a moment, revealing the monster underneath.

Nikolai wasn't about to let this fucker mess with Jun and

get away with it—though he also couldn't just eviscerate enemies right in front of her.

As Ryan turned, waving a goodbye as he strolled out of the store, Nikolai followed.

The second Nikolai stepped out of the store, it was as if the man had disappeared without a trace. Nikolai turned in the direction that Ryan was headed in, but the streets and sidewalk were clear in all directions.

Jogging down the quiet streets, Nikolai searched for any hint of the man. But nothing was out of place. As he got to the end of the block, all the hairs rose on the back of his neck, and he clenched his fist.

Something wasn't right.

It wasn't physically possible to move this fast, and he hadn't seen or smelled any hint of magic.

What if Ryan really couldn't move this quickly? What is there was no sign of him because he simply hadn't moved at all?

What if he was lying in wait, holding off until the perfect opportunity. Like when the trained assassin ran off like an idiot, leaving Jun alone and defenseless in her craft store?

Nikolai pivoted and bolted, sprinting hard all the way back to Jun's store.

Yanking the door open, Nikolai launched into the store, only to skid to a halt at the sight of Jun sitting at the counter hunched over her work binder.

Nikolai let out a deep breath as he ran his hands through his hair.

Jun was safe, for now. But what the hell was that? Jun had the most powerful magic that Nikolai had ever seen, but that didn't mean that she couldn't get hurt. Whoever this Ryan fellow was, he was a threat.

There was no way that this was a coincidence. Magicians

with deadly powers had to have better things to do than single out small businesses to buy some craft supplies.

"Nikolai." Jun pressed two fingers to her temple as if she were staving off a headache. "I appreciate you protecting me. But... is there any way that you could do it without, you know, pulling knives out right in front of my customers?"

"Jun, that man was dangerous."

"You say that about everyone who comes in." Jun rolled her eyes.

All right, so maybe that was true. Jun had thrown a fit when he had admitted to scaring her customers away. Yes, she was still a bit pissed at him. But, guarding her and facing her aggravation was better than the uncertainty of dealing with literal killers having constant access to her, in a confined space with only one exit door.

"He's a magician. I couldn't even track him, the guy vanished almost immediately."

"How do you know that?" Jun's lips pressed together in a tight line. Nikolai would think that she was irritated with him, except that she had become very still.

"It's leftover from whatever that rabbit did to me." Though that furry creature was about as much of a real rabbit as Nikolai himself was. It was a magical entity and it had taken to following Jun around for reasons that escaped Nikolai's understanding. Occasionally popping in and out of impossible places. Jun had asked the white rabbit to heal him a couple of months back. He'd been healed and his eyesight came back, though he could only see in shades of gray.

But no, that wasn't when this started. He'd been able to see the colors of magic before then. Ever since that other one, the darker one had gotten to him. The creature that sometimes took the shape of a black rabbit and sometimes took the shape of a monster. That was what had taken his eyesight. Plucked it right out of his face and left behind whatever this was.

"I can still see magic. That man had it. Looked like he was capable of something nasty. I thought he was going to kill you."

There was no reason to assume that a magician couldn't be behind the prophecy.

Magicians were deadly. Nikolai had dedicated over half his life to taking them down. He had the scars to prove it.

"But he didn't do anything to me. Just bought some yarn." Jun crossed her arms across her chest as she shook her head. "You think he's going to knit some torture device for me?"

Nikolai ran his fingers through his hair, exasperated. "Just take the week off. Shut the store down. Put up a sign that you're closed for renovations. Whatever. You don't need to think about it as going into hiding. Take a vacation. I can get us a great hotel in Hawaii, or France, or wherever you want to go."

Jun drummed her fingers against the top drawer of her register. "What if running away like that is exactly the thing that gets me killed?"

She had a point. *Damn it.*

"What if it isn't?"

If it wasn't, Jun was sitting on her ass like a lamb waiting for the slaughterhouse.

Jun stared off into the distance, as if her window display held all the secrets of the universe.

Nikolai braced himself for whatever sarcastic excuse she'd throw at him next. His mind raced to find a reasonable explanation that would sound reasonable to *her*.

Instead, she bit her lip and locked eyes with him. "Did you mean what you said?"

"Mean what?"

"That you want to go hide in a different country? Together, I mean."

"Yeah? I wouldn't have suggested it if I didn't."

Jun bit her lip. "What are we?"

Oh. That's where she was going with this.

Nikolai swallowed.

They had never discussed this thing that had developed between them. Sure, he'd kissed her. Vowed to protect her. But he had never put into words what he felt.

How could he explain it to her?

She made him feel alive.

He hadn't even realized that he was numb until she had gotten under his skin and made him feel again. Never realized how draining it was to be driven by revenge, chasing after the shadow of memories. As if any amount of bloodshed could bring back the people he'd lost.

And he hadn't realized that what he wanted came in a five-foot package, brimming with sarcasm and an odd knitting fixation, until Jun had dropped into his life like a rabid chipmunk—disrupting everything.

He flexed his fingers, curling and unfurling them, before forcing the words out. "I want to be with you."

"Why would you want to be with someone... like me." *Like a magician.* The unspoken words hung in the air between them.

After spending over a decade hunting down the worst of her kind, it was a magician he had feelings for. It didn't make sense for him to want her.

But he'd seen her. The real her.

Yes, she said stupid shit that grated against his last nerve, but she also broke past all his defenses. After he hadn't gotten close to anyone. Couldn't get close to anyone. He'd been a dead man. A shell. Because before her, he'd lived to put a stop to the people who'd ripped his life apart. To save others from facing the void.

But she made him feel.

Somehow, she'd become everything to him. His reason to smile.

His ridiculous, radiant girl.

"People don't choose who they love," Nikolai said.

"You love me?" Jun asked in a quiet voice.

Oh, *fuck.*

He was going to scare her off before he even got a chance.

Nikolai ran his hand through his hair, trying to figure out what to say to fix this. *But I'll be whatever you let me be. We can be friends. I won't be weird about it.*

It didn't matter if he was with her or not. As long as he could protect her. As long as he knew she was free from whoever was after her. As long as she was okay. If he knew that she was safe, he could live with that.

Jun reached for his hand, placing her slight fingers over his own. Nikolai held his breath, bracing himself for her verdict. Mentally shoring up his defenses, putting together back-up plans for when she turned him down.

Then she was leaning into him, pressing those plush lips against his own.

He kissed her back—his senses filled with the bright floral scent of lavender and the press of slight curves as he held her.

Lovely.

His fingers itched to grasp her tighter, marveling at the fact that he hadn't managed to screw this up.

Nikolai took a shaky breath as he pulled away from her. "So, you wanna get out of here?"

Jun raised an eyebrow. "Like... go back to my place?"

"Or further. We could check out Bali. Some place sunny. Already found tickets for two. We could be on the plane before midnight."

Jun shook her head. "I can't."

Why the hell not? Because a stupid line of destiny told her she couldn't?

"Fuck the prophecy. I can protect you. I've been fighting against magic for most of my life. You don't have to listen to a single word of it. You have me." Nikolai's chest tightened as he clenched his hands to stop himself from grabbing Jun, hurling her over his shoulder like some neanderthal, and running for safety.

She lowered her chin, eyes downcast.

Nikolai sighed. He brushed the back of his knuckle against her cheek. "What is it?"

"This shop—it's what I've been working for all that time in college. It's been my dream since I was just a kid. I can't just throw this all away. I don't want this stupid prophecy to control me."

Nikolai nodded as he pulled her close, holding her.

Wishing all the while that he could rip apart everything binding her here.

CHAPTER 9

"Are you planning on summoning a god" —Samuel shook the contents of the bag— "with breakfast cereal?"

Samuel Brown, head warlock of the Greater Northern Pacific Coven, forced himself not to roll his eyes as he stared helplessly at their offering. The pentagram, assembled out of oak twigs on sacred ground, was still shadowed by a millennia-old Douglas fir. Hooded figures knelt at each star point, and the full moon would soon strike the heart of the sigil. All they were missing was the blood offering.

Which, apparently, Victoria hadn't bothered to get.

Samuel watched the moonlight inch closer to the heart of their star. Light over the dark, on an ancient grove that had stood as civilizations rose and civilizations fell. Magic was practically woven into its roots. It would have to be enough to summon the ancient ones. It had to work. The prophecies were increasingly dire. All the variations hinting at the future agreed—they were running out of time. It had to be tonight. They didn't have time to do this again.

This was an offering to the gods. What the hell was she thinking?

Samuel pressed a finger to his temple. The crux of their entire ritual depended on this offering. Why didn't he just do it himself?

"I told you to get a chicken," Samuel said through gritted teeth.

"That's cruel."

Samuel took a deep, composing breath.

He pulled out a Ziplock bag filled with... Was that Fruit Loops? Or Trix? Samuel pressed his face into his palm. He cast a doubtful look on the light edging closer to their offering site. There wouldn't be enough time to get someone to drive off to Magnolia Ranch and pick up a chicken. There wasn't even enough time to drive to Safeway for one already dispatched.

Samuel sighed. "Why, Victoria?"

"I saw it in a dream," she muttered sheepishly.

Was it possible that Victoria saw through this moment into the great beyond? Her visions had been correct before.

But cereal?

The moonlight reached the edge of their offering site, bathing the first acolyte in an ethereal glow. They were out of time.

They could complete the ritual with cereal, or they could wait a month and do it right. Except that they didn't have a month.

Samuel muttered a curse under his breath as he opened the Ziplock bag, pouring out a handful of cereal in his palm. He pulled out the ceremonial dagger of refined silver and held it high to catch the moonlight. He delicately slashed the cereal, imagining very hard that it was a chicken instead.

He scattered the offering across the pentagram as moonlight swept over the forest floor.

"Great Ancient One." Samuel imbued his words with intention, gathering his magic. They needed help. The very world needed help. "The children of the earth, practitioners of magic, summon you. We cry out to you, ancient god of the land, imploring you to come to us in our hour of need."

Samuel raised both hands in supplication and surrender. It was up to the will of the gods now.

The acolytes stopped their chanting, and a hush fell over the forest.

Samuel gazed into the pentagram, straight into the eyes of the god—in the form of a humble creature of the earth. Pure, unadulterated magic. Though he wore white fur and had the body of a rabbit, it did little to disguise his power. Positively humming, the air was charged with the electrifying weight of it.

The white rabbit, god of light, met Samuel's gaze.

Samuel swallowed, recognizing those eyes. Though he had never successfully summoned the Old One before, this wasn't the first time he had seen those eyes.

In Samuel's brightest moments, did he not see those same eyes? Basking in his successes. Shining a path for hope in his dismal failures. Unfailing, unending.

The Ancient One was always in his life, waiting for him. Waiting for this moment.

"Ancient One," Samuel whispered, awed.

The god stepped toward their offering, picking up a piece of cereal in both paws. He sniffed it delicately and ate it.

An awed silence took over the grove, as Samuel, the acolytes and even nature itself held its breath.

"We seek your counsel, wise one. Prophecies speak of

coming destruction. We seek the aid of the most powerful practitioner of magic to help push back against this catastrophe."

The ancient god perked one ear up in response. He hopped to the center of the pentagram and thumped one hind leg against the glass.

An image stirred within the depths of the glass—a reflection from beyond. Magic was rooted to the earth, yet it broke those binds, pulling from the essence and spirit of things, transcending reality. Overcoming the physical confines of reality, magic was limitless.

The reflection sharpened and colors emerged, settling into the form of a bright purple hat. A hat on a girl who sat on a bench, knitting.

"She is the most powerful magic wielder?" Samuel raised an eyebrow. He turned to look at Victoria at her spot at the right of the pentagram, but she just shrugged at him.

No help from fate then.

The girl didn't look like an advanced magic user—or someone who used magic at all for that matter. She showed no clear signs of wear from the use of dark magic. In all honesty it just didn't feel right for someone powerful to go about their day in bright knitted apparel.

Samuel opened his mouth to ask the Ancient One for clarification. Not that Samuel would question his wisdom, but there had to be something he wasn't seeing here.

But the Ancient One was already gone.

The others surrounded the pentagram, watching the image in the glass as the colors lost their vibrancy and the girl began to fade.

"Look, there's a business card, half-buried under the yarn." Tessa pointed.

"Xochitl, quick, you're closest. What does it say?" Nova

leaned as close to the reflection as she could without leaving her point on the pentagram.

Xochitl gazed into the image, even after the girl with the purple hat completely vanished and the glass reflected the shapes of the forest once more.

"It says Get Crafty," Xochitl read.

The acolytes looked at one another and looked at Samuel for answers.

Get Crafty? What in the world did that mean?

CHAPTER 10

Lightning flashed, loud enough to make Sonia squeak and pull the covers to her chin, knocking her bowl of popcorn onto the floor in a metal clatter. Half-buried in fleece, Sonia heard the hum of electricity faltering and stopping as the power went out in the house. The TV clicked off, and her episode of *The Bachelor* blacked out. Everything went dark.

Sonia rooted around her in pockets and turned on her cell phone. The light of it pierced through the gloom. Twenty percent. Why hadn't she charged it? How long would twenty percent last if she turned the flashlight on? Sonia wasn't sure, but it probably wasn't too long.

Sonia held her phone's flashlight up and cast a thin ray of light over the room. This wasn't going to cut it.

If I were a flashlight, where would I be?

Sonia got off the sofa, stepping on bits of popcorn, and looked around for the likely hiding spot for a candle or a match or something. Ryan, her boyfriend, would know where it was, but he was probably driving back home now.

Sonia didn't want to distract him when it was already rainy and miserable out on the road.

The flashlight on her phone illuminated a tiny circle in the darkness. There was a filing cabinet by the desk. Sonia opened it but found nothing but paperwork.

She walked slowly to the kitchen, padding barefoot across the cold tiles. Opening drawers, she found the spare can opener and a pair of scissors that had disappeared a few weeks ago. Well, she could cross off 'buy new scissors' from her mental checklist. Not that it helped her now.

Sonia checked her phone battery. Thirteen percent.

This was ridiculous.

Ryan kept all sorts of tools in the garage. If there was a flashlight in the house, that was where it would be. He'd warned her not to go in the garage—sweet of him, really. Too many tools lying about on that car project he was tinkering with. He didn't want her to get hurt. Well, this was clearly an emergency. Ryan would understand.

Ryan was nothing at all like her last boyfriend. What was she even thinking with that cheating piece of—anyway. Ryan really knew how to take care of a girl. Remembered her birthday. Got her the good flowers for Valentine's Day. A dozen red roses. None of those wilted six-dollar bouquets like her ex got her as a flimsy apology. Date night every Friday. He'd take her somewhere classy. Ryan was really too good to be true.

Sonia opened the door to the garage and stepped inside, the hair on her arms prickling and a chill running down her spine as the temperature dropped twenty degrees. She swept her phone's light about in wide swaths, revealing the red of a Ford Thunderbird with the hood up, diamond-plate flooring and a metal toolbox. Bingo.

Pointing her phone's light down at the floor—she didn't

want to step on a nail or some other car thing—Sonia padded across the garage and unlatched the toolbox.

Sonia looked in the first compartment for the flashlight when the sight of something odd gave her pause.

Why was there a syringe in the toolbox?

She shook her head. It had to be some kind of car thing? Like maybe to inject oil into tight places? Or something? Ryan would never have something like this to hurt someone —he wasn't like that.

But the sight of it caused Sonia to look more closely at the contents of the toolbox. Next to the syringe was a little vial. She leaned in closer, squinting to read the label. Rohypnol? What the hell was that? Could that be for allergies? If her phone wasn't at thirteen percent, she would have stopped everything and searched it up.

Right. The phone percentage. The flashlight. It was not a good idea to search for a flashlight in pitch darkness.

Sonia opened the second compartment of the toolbox. Lying neatly in the partitions were all the expected tools, like a hammer, some screwdrivers, adjustable wrench, measuring tape, screws in neat boxes. Oh. A flashlight. Not that she was searching for anything else that wasn't supposed to be there. What else could there be?

Stop it. There had to be a reasonable explanation for the syringe in the toolbox. Sonia must simply have been freaked out by the power outage.

Hands shaking, Sonia flicked on the flashlight. She sighed as light flooded the dank space turning off the one on her phone. Seven? It had gone all the way down to seven percent? At five, her phone shut off completely. She had found the flashlight just in the nick of time.

Sonia turned to get out of the garage and flinched at the image painted on the side of the Thunderbird. It was a faint gray outline of a woman's face, with a gaping mouth and eyes wide with terror—eyes that felt like they were staring straight at her.

Leaning closer to the image, Sonia held her breath as her heartbeat raced. The painting looked awfully familiar. Just like that co-worker of Ryan's. Erin. Didn't she move away a week or so back?

Why paint her on his car? Why paint anything on his car?

What was with that creepy expression?

Sonia gulped. Did she even want to know?

Was not knowing worse?

Almost as if she were pulled without her consent, without conscious thought, Sonia stepped closer to the hood of the Thunderbird. Inside, the motor looked normal at first. But under the wires and panels was a little metal hand, reaching out. Stretching as if it had tried and failed to escape, the fingernails were chipped and painted red.

It looked so life-like.

Tentatively, Sonia placed one finger against the odd little hand. It was cool to the touch, but soft. Not at all the texture of metal. It almost felt like it was...

The metal finger twitched.

Sonia retracted her hand like it burned, clutching it to her chest.

What did it mean? None of this was making any sense. There had to be some kind of reasonable explanation. What in the hell was going on?

Sonia stumbled back with a gasp, nearly dropping the flashlight with how hard her hand was shaking.

"What are you doing in here?"

Sonia spun, pointing her flashlight like it was a weapon.

It was just Ryan. She hadn't heard him open the door.

Obviously, she couldn't see him enter behind her in the pitch black.

The rain had splattered across his broad shoulders and drenched the curls in his dark hair. His jaw was set, mouth frozen in a firm line.

Sonia clenched the flashlight like a lifeline as her stomach turned rock hard. Why was he looking at her like that? She hadn't done anything wrong.

"The power went out," Sonia practically whispered.

Ryan sighed. "I told you it wasn't safe for you to come in here."

Sonia shook her head. Why did that matter? She wasn't hurt. She could have gotten hurt alone in the darkness. "I didn't know what to do."

"Just one little request. All I've ever asked of you." Ryan smiled the crooked smile that Sonia loved. It didn't reach his eyes.

"Not." Ryan took a step closer to her.

"To go." Closer.

"Into the garage."

He stepped right into the light of the flashlight. "Why couldn't you just listen?"

Ryan's shadow was all wrong—arching up from beyond his back, thin and twitching like the legs of a spider.

Ryan shook his head. "You *really* should have listened to me."

CHAPTER 11

Marco Russo held his hands folded as his fellow assassins huddled together, bowing their heads in prayer and supplication as they called on a higher power to intervene.

Marco opened his eyes after a moment, knowing that no one else in his team would open theirs and do the same—he was the only atheist. Not that the other others knew about his religious beliefs or lack thereof. He stared up at the popcorn ceiling of their rented apartment, willing himself not to shift his feet against the creaky hardwood.

Just stop fidgeting.

A year ago, Marco would have laughed at their efforts. Not anymore. Not after all he'd seen. Now, he was half-convinced that there was something to their faith. Whatever it was that they were doing, it was working.

Not that it mattered.

He'd joined the northwest contingent of the Holy Order of Saint Christopher to kill magicians, after all. Their methods might not have made sense, but Marco wasn't one to argue with the results. Or the payout.

Don't fixate on the money; it's going to mess you up.

But rumor had it that Nikolai Visiliev was retired. Not that Marco had anything against the guy. They'd worked with him half a year back. He was professional. Too professional. One of those that was driven to the extreme. According to the record books, Visiliev had taken down more magicians than anyone currently working for the Order. And the guy was only in his mid-twenties.

Problem was he tended to go off on his own, following clues. More often than not, he'd end up finishing magicians on his own—earning him the majority of the bounty awarded by the church. Which was exactly what ended up happening when Visiliev had worked with Marco's team.

The thing was, Visiliev didn't even seem like he cared about the money at *all*. He seemed more driven by a personal vendetta to kill as many magicians as he could get his hands on. With Visiliev out of the picture, there were more magicians out there for the rest of the Order to tackle.

Meanwhile, Marco just needed one more takedown with his team. One more bounty, from one of the more deadly classes of magician, and Marco would have enough to pay off his sister's medical bills.

Marco couldn't believe that her fucking doctor refused further treatment until her outstanding charges were paid off. How the hell was she supposed to pay when she was too sick to provide for herself?

Come on, focus.

Giovanni De Luca sighed deeply as he began to pray. His words were melodious, flowing with a deep baritone. "Dear Lord, I pray for your guidance. I pray for your protection and power over those who practice sorcery and the darkest arts. Help me to protect people from the wicked. In Jesus's name, Amen."

Marco muttered a hasty "Amen" as the others opened their eyes and waited solemnly. A tense thirty seconds passed in silence.

Lightning flashed, brilliant and near, and thunder ripped through the air.

Sparks crackled from the power lines, and the lights went dead. As the power ground to a halt, a broomstick leaning against the wall slid to the ground in a clatter. Marco stood with his hands crossed as his team observed the fallen broomstick, praising the Lord for his sign and blessing.

Marco raised an eyebrow. Well, they certainly had never taken the advice of humble household appliances before. So this was new.

"It's pointing south toward Main Street," Giovanni said, his hand an inch above the plastic bristles.

All the signs panning out were almost enough to turn an atheist into a believer—if they weren't also fighting against the forces of magic. If nothing else, his training taught him not to trust phenomena that he couldn't understand. No matter how much the others might believe it, there was no evidence that their help came from a benevolent god.

Marco patted the meteorite iron blade at his holster. Standard issue to new recruits. Wasn't as pretty as the heirloom piece Giovanni carried and nicknamed the Little Rod of Iron. The Order of Saint Christopher had an impressive stockpile of meteorite and had contracts to process out the iron. They even had bullets made out of the stuff. Logan stashed a few in a leather pouch and never traveled without it.

Meteorite iron was one of the few substances that canceled out magic. Weaker magic, anyway.

As they headed out of their shared apartment, rain lashed down, piercing through Marco's thin jacket. Wind howled as they walked through the gloom. The streetlights were down, and though full, the light of the moon was obscured in clouds.

Giovanni took the lead, heading south. Following divine instructions sent to the earth through the mighty fall of cleaning supplies.

The team walked down Main Street, surrounded on both sides by squat, miniature houses that still managed to cost twice as much as the national average. They were surrounded by chain link fences that enclosed front yards all covered with weeds. Marco swore that he saw a chicken in one of the backyards, and the nearest farm was miles away.

Marco shook his head, hoping it looked like he was just trying to dislodge some raindrops. He hoped that God's mighty broomstick was leading them to the right place and that they weren't walking through a shady neighborhood filled with chickens and who knew what else for no good reason.

They were three blocks into their walk down Main Street before they heard the scream. One lone cry of fear and surprise. It wasn't a coincidence. It never was.

"There." Demetrius pointed to a small ranch house directly adjacent to them. Demetrius had a sixth sense for hunting down magicians like he was some kind of coonhound on steroids.

The team went into action.

Logan crouched low to the ground, aiming his pistol at the windows, while Demetrius and Giovanni headed to the door. Marco walked to the garage door, giving it a tug. Locked. He unlatched the fence and noted a side door. Finding it unlocked, Marco pushed his way in.

Illuminated by a shaky flashlight, a stocky man had his

hands wrapped around a woman's throat, pressing her backwards into the hood of a car. His eyes as he looked up and met Marco's gaze were all wrong—pupils constricted into tight points, sharp and razor-focused. Marco had seen that look before.

Now's your chance. One quick jab to the throat. Finish him yourself and take all the payout.

Yes, and mess up and leave his little sister all alone in the world. Without treatment and drowning in medical bills she had no hope of paying off.

The memory of Izzy in the hospital—pale and covered in tubes, her eyes too large in her emaciated body—flashed through his mind, distracting him.

The element of surprise was gone. Marco missed his chance.

"Garage!" Marco called, alerting the others as he drew his blade.

Standard procedure was to wait for the others, and normally Marco would have done that. Maybe he could blame it on that leftover internal voice screaming at himself to finish the magician on his own. Or, if he was being honest with himself, there was just something about the way the man had his hands around that poor slip of a girl that made his blood boil.

Marco charged in, darting into the dark depths of the room, as the magician dropped the girl and lunged after him. Turning sharply, Marco moved behind the car, as if they were playing a lethal game of keep away. His eyes darted to the girl as she gasped for breath. Four steps to the right and he could position himself in front of her.

The magician yanked a shovel off its shelving hook and pivoted it in his hands. The metal flickered with a pulse of light that rippled across its surface. He held it high like a sword.

Marco eyed the glowing metal warily. "What's with the shovel? Were wands out of stock at the local magic emporium?"

The magician curled his lip, baring teeth like a predator, before he charged.

The tip of the blunted metal sliced through the air in an arc. Marco stepped back to avoid it, but not far enough away that he couldn't feel how the blade heated the air, sizzling and crackling in the space where he had just been standing.

Well, that wasn't good. Yeah, that was a magic shovel. Touching that was not on the agenda for the day. He'd have to stall for time. Just needed to wait long enough for the others to make their way to him. They couldn't be far. Unless they were somewhere in the house or backyard and couldn't hear him? But even then, their search through the house would eventually bring them back here.

Marco dropped low, kicking out and catching the magician's legs as he tried to dart back. The magician stumbled and the shovel hit the ground in a cloud of sparks like striking hot embers.

Marco held his knife in a hammer grip, slicing at the air in front of him.

But the magician righted himself and swung the shovel in an arc. With one sharp swipe of his blade, Marco deflected the blow, letting the shovel slide past him.

Just then the door slammed open, and Marco let out the breath he was holding in. He called out to his team. "Watch out, he's got a magic shovel."

The assassins of the Holy Order of Saint Christopher stepped out of the shadow and surrounded the magician, who looked around wildly, taking them all in. The magician raised his shovel high and slammed it against the floor of the garage. The ground beneath them rippled, as if it were no longer quite solid. Before Marco had time to react, Giovanni knelt to the ground, plunging the rod of iron into the garage flooring. As the magic canceled out, the waves abruptly leveled off. It remained still as Giovanni got to his feet, pulling the blade from the floor as nobly as King Arthur releasing his sword from stone.

As one, the assassins of the Order attacked. Marco kicked out once again, tripping the magician. Before he could right himself, Giovanni was on top of him, knife at his throat. Demetrius slashed his blade at the shovel, sending it clattering into the far wall in a shower of sparks.

"See to the victim," Giovanni said, eyes locked on the magician.

The girl, who had been hidden in the shadows, was slight and fair. Marco knelt beside her slowly, careful not to make any sudden movements. He checked her for injuries while she quivered like a butterfly. Dark bruises covered her neck in the distinct shape of a handprint.

The girl bit her lip as she gazed across the room, looking directly into the car hood.

Marco followed the path of her gaze and stared blankly at the car engine—until he saw the hand emerging from beneath wires and metal. "We got a second victim here," he called.

"I won't kill you," Giovanni vowed, pressing the tip of his knife tighter against the magician's jaw, "if you free the one you've wronged."

The magician raised his arms in a sign of submission. "Fine. If that's what you want," he muttered.

As Demetrius dragged him to his feet, Marco tightened his grip on his own weapon.

Knife still pressed against his neck, the magician approached the car. Then he pushed his arm into the engine. The metal rippled around his body like it was water or some kind of mirage. He shifted around as if he were reaching for something. After a moment, his arm went taut as he braced his body against the ground, wrenching and tugging. From the car engine, he hauled out a petite hand—though it was oddly metallic and covered in car grease. The magician tugged sharply, and then a crumpled body emerged. It tumbled over the front bumper of the car.

Giovanni dove after the victim, catching the body before it could fall, at the exact same time that the magician leapt. He dove into the metal, completely disappearing into the car engine.

Demetrius charged after him, his body slamming into the metal of the car, denting the side panels.

Behind them, the car roared to life, just as the garage door clanked open.

Demetrius stood his ground, blocking the exit. The car edged forward, daring them to act.

A shot rang out and a bullet lodged into the rubber garage tiles. Right in the spot where the car tires sat a moment before.

Headlights flashed on. The tires squealed and the Thunderbird reversed out of the garage. Demetrius leapt out of the way, slashing his blade along the side in a shower of sparks. The car engine roared as it raced down the street and into the night. Just some careless driver, unless anyone was close enough to see that there was no one sitting in the driver's seat. The car was driving all on its own.

Their kill count would be higher if Giovanni wasn't so fixated on protecting the victims.

Not that Marco didn't want to save people. Obviously,

they should help them... but this was the third time that their culprit had gotten away.

It was the one thing about the team that annoyed him.

The pulse of the victim fluttered like a hummingbird as Marco helped her to her feet. He understood. Lives were more important than the payout.

But knowing that did nothing to help his sister—being a hero sure didn't pay the bills.

The grease-covered woman they had pulled out of the car had her eyes screwed shut and was whimpering on the garage floor. Giovanni held his fingers to the woman's neck. "Weak pulse. She's too cold." He shook his head and pulled out his phone, hitting three buttons. "Get an ambulance over here. I'll text over the address."

Marco stared at the tire tracks the Thunderbird had left as they were covered by the rain and disappeared.

He felt numb.

"He got away," Marco said, stating the obvious.

How much longer was it going to take him to get the money together?

How much longer could his sister wait?

Giovanni narrowed his eyes at the path the Thunderbird had taken. "No. We got his number now. We'll enter his abilities into the registry. He won't last long."

CHAPTER 12

Two days.

How did she only have two days left?

Don't think about it. Don't panic. It's not going to help. Besides, you still have two days.

Jun strummed her fingers along her register. She'd gone for a retro vintage cash register from the 1950s. More than a pop of color, the thing was a mint green monster. She'd actually found it at an estate sale for fifteen dollars back in high school, and she'd crammed it into the back of her closet for the day that she would have her own store.

Jun half-wished that she had woken Nikolai up. He had crashed on her sofa after staying up to an ungodly hour guarding her house. He was convinced that intruders were going to come for her in the dead of the night.

Jun had taken one look at him, sprawled and snoring on her cramped living room sofa, and decided to let him sleep.

He'd probably wake up annoyed at her. Scratch that. Jun was certain that he would wake up annoyed at her. But what he was doing couldn't be healthy. Wasn't sleep deprivation a form of torture?

Jun knitted at the register as she kept track of the customers. They had arrived early in the morning, just a few minutes after she opened. Two girls. So similar that they could have been twins.

The two girls came in ten minutes apart and didn't acknowledge one another, but they were clearly related. Though one was blonde and the other had jet-black hair, they had the same features—from the structure of their cheek bones to their button noses, all the way to the shape of their chins. They almost looked identical save for their coloration.

They circled through the aisles of the store, looking closely and with apparently a deep fascination at her stacks of yarn and stationery.

Fine. Jun could appreciate a love for crafts. But they had lingered. They'd stuck around the store for three hours so far. There were only so many times that you could make a loop around a craft store. No one was that indecisive. And anyway, it wasn't like Jun had that much in the way of inventory. Her stuff was nice. True. But the girls had circled each item at least four times already.

And out of the corner of her eyes, she noticed that they watched her when it seemed she wasn't looking. Brief, hard stares that Jun felt to her core. They watched her as if she were a lion at the zoo and the pair of them were waiting for her to wake up and roar. Charge the cage. Bite into a piece of meat. Rip into some squirrel or something that got within reach.

Those glances were a bit unnerving. What was it that Nikolai said? That if he were using dark magic to get to her, he would definitely take a shape that she wasn't expecting.

Jun was half tempted to call Nikolai.

Except that he would flip out. There was no way that he

wouldn't panic and cause a scene. Really, these were customers. Customers were supposed to always be right and all of that jazz.

What if this was all stuff she had just made up inside of her head? It wasn't like they were doing anything illegal. It wasn't a crime to browse items in a store and look at someone.

Just then her phone vibrated.

Oh, goody. He was awake. This wasn't going to go over well.

She jammed her fingers into her pocket, digging out her phone as fast as she could without looking like she was grabbing it as fast as she could.

Jun wiped imaginary sweat off her face before she answered the call.

"Hello."

"Jun! Are you okay? Where are you? Please don't tell me you're at the store alone."

"I'm fine. Yes, I'm at the store. No, I'm not alone. Got some customers."

"Shit." His voice sounded half-panicked. "I'm on my way."

He hung up.

Jun sighed.

She stared at her phone as if it were capable of talking and had personally offended her. Jun shook her head. It wasn't her phone's fault that her bodyguard-boyfriend hybrid had a chip loose in his brain.

Whatever. Two days. Two more days and this would be all over one way or another.

Jun bit her lip and then went back to knitting a new row furiously. She had to pause and unravel it because she'd knit the new row too tight.

All the while, the twins lingered. Watching her. The weight of their combined gazes felt heavier now that she knew that Nikolai would shortly come into the store and exactly what he would likely say about it.

In the time it took her to fix her row and add on two more, the entrance chimes sounded. Nikolai burst through her door, skidding to a stop. All windswept hair and teeth clenched in a feral grimace. Like he was ready to rip someone apart with his bare hands.

He paused and looked around the room, noting the twins, who had frozen. The blonde one held a floral sticker packet in hand.

Nikolai scowled as he locked eyes on Jun. He prowled up to the front of the room, and Jun mentally prepared for him to start complaining about her recklessness, or whatever.

She felt it like an electric charge. The energy of it started to swirl and coil around, thickening in the air.

A chill went down her spine, as if the temperature within her had dropped suddenly by thirty degrees. The air tightened, the same way pressure increased when she dove into deeper water. Jun felt like she had been dropped into a pool. All around her, the air pressed tight. Swirling and intensifying. Suffocating.

What was happening?

Nikolai froze, locking his gaze on the girls.

Wind rustled from within the still air of the store, howling and intense. It swiftly picked up, rotating faster, and the knitting needles and stationery rattled against their displays.

Magic.

Black smoke erupted from the palm of the blonde twin. It swirled into a tornado and headed straight for them.

Before Jun could even react, Nikolai scooped her up and

leapt out of the way. There was a heavy crash—a metal display case slammed into the area where Nikolai and Jun had stood. Her cash register toppled over, cracking into the glass display case.

Yarn balls and stationery paper were strewn about in the air as the wind picked up in a fury.

In a move too fast for her eyes to follow, Nikolai grasped his blade from within a hidden panel in his sleeve and threw it.

His knife sailed through the air, aimed straight at the blonde twin. Jun's display table swept fully upright in the rush of wind, as if the hands of an invisible giant had grabbed it and yanked it up. The blur of metal might have been too fast for Jun to see, but the handle of the blade was clear as day, embedded in the vintage table.

She stared at it dully.

Even with her hand clutched to her chest and heart thudding, Jun couldn't take her eyes away from the damage.

Nikolai set her down and attempted to muscle his way past the gust of wind as her imported silk fabric was torn off the metal clips, adding to the chaos. He gritted his teeth as he fought to reclaim his throwing knife.

The last thing she needed was to get blood all over her entire stock of yarn.

Okay. That does it.

Jun sunk to her knees, placing her palms to the floor. Her fury at seeing the inventory she had painstakingly arranged all scattered about clouded her eyes. Jun saw red.

Her head cooled as power settled over her like a well-worn jacket. She sunk all of that anger down deep into the earth, like sinking into warm bath water.

She snapped her eyes open, pulling power from the well of her anger, from the earth itself.

Her magic circled around the twin. Testing. Probing. Meticulously, she wrapped layers of it around, weaving it in a complex web like one of her elaborate crochet patterns. Jun opened her mouth in a slight smile as she felt the connection click into place. Locking around the twin, binding as manacles.

Jun gave her a *SHOVE*.

She slammed her against the window. The twin shattered the glass as her body rocketed out of the store. Shards burst out, glinting in the air and raining down to the ground with the sound of a delicate tinkling.

Jun spread her arms wide as she stared down the swirling mass of her inventory.

I've got to stop this.

Her own wind rippled up, smothering down the rush of spinning craft items—stopping them in an instant. They hung suspended in the air. Completely frozen. Completely still. Her product floated, motionless; a photo brought to life in three dimensions. As if she had stopped time itself.

Wait.

Shit, did I stop time?

Again?

CHAPTER 13

Yarn balls hung suspended in the air like constellations in the sky. Utter silence so ultimate, so complete, that Nikolai could hear his blood pounding in his veins. Hear his lungs expand and contract. Every move that he made was loud against the void. The world around him was confining. Silent. A cage.

It was a feeling that shouldn't have been so familiar to him.

Jun had stopped time.

Not this again.

Creatures lurked here behind the shadows and in the time between time. And that thing, built out of the darkness, with features that bubbled in and out. The creature with too many eyes. Too many limbs. Echoes of scars itched across Nikolai's non-dominant hand. Memories ached beneath his skin.

Nikolai took a deep breath to steady himself, to ward off the nausea brewing in the pit of his stomach. How long had he spent frozen in utter silence the last time Jun stopped time?

He gave himself a mental shake.

Focus.

Jun's killers could still be out there. If she dragged him along for the ride without making direct contact with him, she could have brought someone else into this hellscape.

They could be hiding out anywhere in all of this mess. The blonde intruder was outside, arched over backward as she was flung out of the store. Her face was frozen in open-mouthed surprise. She hadn't even hit the ground yet.

He could end it all now. It would be simple enough. Drive his knife between the fourth and fifth ribs. Straight into the heart, stop it while it was already stopped. If he did it now, in the time between time, she wouldn't even feel a thing.

But what if this wasn't the killer after Jun? The one that they'd been warned about? Could he really dispatch Jun's problem two days early and be done with it?

Or would killing the wrong person be the exact catalyst to bring about Jun's murder?

Would it instill in someone the need for revenge?

Fuck.

Nikolai hated prophecies.

The sound of sniffling jolted him out of his thoughts.

Jun stood in the center of the store, in the same spot where she had unleashed her magic. All the merchandise hung frozen and half-destroyed all around her. She was struggling not to cry.

Loose at her sides, her hands were shaking. It was an after-effect from all that high powered magic running through her system. Nikolai caught her fingers with his own and stroked his thumb along her wrist. Warming her with his touch.

Even with her eyes red-rimmed and glistening with unshed tears, Jun was the loveliest girl he'd ever seen.

A perfect heart shaped face. Those dark, doe-like eyes.

He never stood a chance against her.

Jun clenched her eyes tight as if that could shut out the sadness that pooled under her lashes and slid down to her chin.

"This is just stuff. You can replace it." One of his calloused fingers traced against the curve of her cheek, gently brushing away the wet trails left behind by her tears. "The only thing in this store that's irreplaceable is you."

His hands laced into the silky strands of her dark hair as he leaned in and caught her lips against his. Wanting nothing but to lose himself in her sweet touch and the soft press of skin against skin. He allowed himself a brief moment of contact before reluctantly pulling away.

Jun burrowed against his chest, sniffling harder. "I didn't mean to."

Nikolai pulled her into a hug, brushing a kiss against the top of her head. "We got out of it once; we can figure this out again."

Jun shook her head. "Even if I can figure out how to get time to go back to normal, I've screwed everything up. The store is a mess. I used magic when I wasn't supposed to. I don't know what I'm going to do."

"You aren't in this alone." He held her in his arms, letting his senses fill with the beating of her heart, her deep calming breaths. Holding her tight enough to embrace this entire moment, where she was safe. She was here. And he wasn't going to let anything happen to her.

"Maybe you're right," Jun sighed. "Maybe we should just get away from here."

Nikolai didn't say a word. He tensed with anticipation,

not wanting to say something that would ruin Jun's abrupt change of heart.

Maybe if I say nothing, she'll talk herself into leaving with me.

Things might finally be looking up. A vacation rather than dealing with killers. She could file a police report and go off to Jamaica on holiday with him. Deal with the mess and rebuild when they got back.

Nikolai felt a pressure appear on his head.

He froze stock still, every muscle in his body tensed, as adrenaline slammed through his veins. Slowly, he looked up. The dark eyes of a fluffy menace looked back at him.

It was Jun's rabbit.

More precisely, it was the being that presented itself in the shape of the rabbit.

But that wasn't all that it was.

Nikolai's other senses awakened. When he closed his eyes, he could see the outline of what it truly was. The creature burned bright as a supernova. A sun in miniature. A god on earth.

What the hell does it want now?

"Hey, you," Jun crooned, holding her hand out to the thing. The white rabbit jumped to her outstretched palm and allowed Jun to wrap her arms around it and hug it like some all-powerful stuffed animal. "You caught us at a bad time. I just ruined everything. I trashed the store you told me to make." Her eyes turned watery again.

She sighed, burying her head into white fur. "And apparently there are a bunch of killers that are supposed to come after me in two days."

The rabbit flicked an ear up at that, as if it was news to him.

"I don't think that insurance is even going to cover this. I can't write on the form that some crazed magical person set off a tornado in my store." She ran her fingers through her hair.

"Can you help me?" She turned to the rabbit.

The little guy perked up, nodding vigorously.

Jun let him down and he hopped to the floor, circling the mess inquisitively. Her silk hung in shredded tatters. Display signs and price tags that Jun had spent weeks agonizing over with graphs and excel spreadsheets were all over the place. Somewhere along the way, a container of glitter had burst open, coating all the carnage in the store with a light dusting of sparkles.

The rabbit thumped his hind leg down hard.

The mess shimmered as if the glitter all got caught in the light, burning with brightness, encased in the light. Then it started to move. The objects rearranged themselves. The glass shards picked themselves off of the floor, floating their way back to the broken window. They arranged themselves back into the gilded lettering of 'Get Crafty.' The yarn balls toppled down to the floor and hopped back into their baskets and piles. The table righted itself. With a noise like a wet cork pulled out of a wine bottle, the dent from the knife mark was yanked out, leaving behind a smooth wooden surface. Displays stacked themselves up into a tower. The haze of glitter coalesced into a thick sparkling cloud and spiraled back in a corkscrew pattern, all fluttering back into its container. Once it was filled, it snapped close with a pop.

Once Jun's store was more or less put back together again, the rabbit hopped to the table, bowing low as if he were on center stage accepting applause.

Fine. That furball could weasel his way into Jun's good side. As long as he was solving problems for her rather than causing a new host of them.

"Now I don't have to report this!" Jun sniffed loudly, her eyes shining bright. "I was worried that I might even have to shut down permanently."

The rabbit's expression turned grave. More solemn an expression than should have been physically possible on a small furry mammal. He looked Jun right in the eyes and shook his head in a firm no.

"No?" Jun asked in a small voice. "What do you mean?"

The rabbit fixed an intense stare at her.

She ran her fingers through her hair nervously. "Is it safer for me to stay here?"

The rabbit blinked at her slowly, as if that little motion was depicting centuries of wise advice. Then he hopped on to the table behind Jun's display.

Nikolai walked after the little guy, but he was gone. Disappeared into thin air.

After cleaning up the store Jun built for him, the rabbit hopped along his merry way, ignoring the whole frozen in time issue.

That little shit.

What did he mean, no? No, Jun. Don't get to safety. Just keep risking your life, and for what? To sell crafting merchandise?

His first real relationship and he was doing nothing while his girl flirted with danger. There was a literal prophecy warning her that killers were after her. And he was just sitting there, letting a fucking rabbit convince her that she should stick around, right in harm's way.

"Jun, I still think that we should get out of here."

"But the rabbit warned me not to leave." Jun frowned. She waved a hand at the store, all patched up like the whirlwind attack was nothing more than a bad dream. "He fixed up the store and everything."

"You're taking the advice of a rabbit? Over me?"

"It's a magic rabbit."

"Still."

Jun bit her lip, taking in a shaky breath. "It's not just the rabbit. It's my prophecy. The last time I ignored a prophecy, I got us both trapped and it almost killed us. Both of us. What if I'm risking that again?"

What if you're not? Nikolai bit his tongue. Arguing wasn't going to get him anywhere with Jun. She'd stubbornly dig her heels in until it was impossible to get her to see reason. "Let's just take this one step at a time. We've got to figure out how to end this magic. Then we can plan on what to do next."

"Okay. Then I just need to word this right in my head." Jun tapped her finger against her lip.

"What were you thinking to activate the magic in the first place?"

"Uhh. That I didn't want you to get blood on my yarn stock?"

"What? What does that have to do with anything?" Nikolai shook his head. They were getting off track.

"I don't know. I don't have every thought that has ever gone through my head memorized."

"All of this happened like five minutes ago. You can't remember what you were thinking five minutes ago?" Nikolai pinched his nose and closed his eyes.

"Just let me think." Jun wrung her hands together. "Hey, is my yarn by the cash register?"

Nikolai prowled over to her cash register, grasping the yarn ball and knitting needles. It was stuck in place as if it were frozen there. Nikolai wrapped his arm tight around the yarn ball, jerking his hand up. The yarn resisted, for a moment staying frozen in place. Nikolai tugged it as if he were hauling up a fifty-pound weight. Once he held it closer to himself, the yarn ball lightened up, feeling like it was less than half of a pound. He dragged her knitting project—some scarf—off her desk and handed it to Jun.

Jun muttered thanks. She began to knit, weaving the yarn in a quick rhythm.

She was halfway through the row when she met Nikolai's eyes with a sharp gasp. "Oh, wait, now I remember. I was thinking that I needed to stop this. When I was worried about you killing that intruder in my store."

"That's it?

"Yeah?"

"You just thought that you wanted this to stop and time stopped for you?"

"I think so."

"All right. Then if you try the opposite, if you think that you want time to restart, maybe it will."

"I guess I could try that." Jun bit her lip, staring at her palms and curling her fingers inward.

"Wait." Nikolai pointed to the frozen girl, paused in the middle of her ejection out the window. "Before you do that. We need to come up with a plan about her."

"Oh, right. The twin."

"Twin?" Something dropped in the pit of his stomach. "What do you mean 'twin'? I just saw this one." Nikolai pointed to the girl Jun had magically tossed out the window.

Jun pressed her index finger into her forehead, as if she had a headache as she screwed her eyes shut tight. After what felt like too long, she looked up at him.

"I don't know." She met his gaze, wide-eyed. "I couldn't even tell you what she looks like. I'm sure that I'm supposed to know it, but it feels like the information was scrubbed from my brain."

"Then it's some sort of magic and there is another attacker out there. You said it was a girl?" One of them was capable of creating tornadoes that were at least at a Level Two supernatural power. The one who was still out there was able to wipe out the knowledge that Jun had even seen her. She was still out there. Possibly even listening to their entire conversation.

"Do you think we should kill her?" Jun eyed the dagger in his palm. His heirloom blade passed down through generations of hunters of magic users. A blade that had seen the end of all kinds of dark magicians through the years. Nikolai had had other blades commissioned, forged of meteorite iron, the only substance that could stop the spread of magic. Generally, it was his heirloom blade that made it into his palm. The blade he took out when he was ready to complete a kill. For some reason, it just felt natural in his hands.

Back when he thought that he knew everything there was to know about magic, he would have plunged that knife between her frozen ribs and taken out the threat. He wouldn't even have thought about it.

That felt like another life.

Now he had no idea which move was the right one. Like he was on a tightrope, walking the thin line that could keep Jun safe. That was the worst thing about prophecy. All the second guessing himself. Would avoiding the prophecy be the thing to bring it about? Or was ignoring it completely the surefire way to bring killers to Jun's doorstep? What about putting down a potential killer and getting it wrong? While her sister stood in silent witness to how they hunted a defenseless person down.

Even though she'd ripped Jun's store apart, why didn't she feel like a threat? He didn't feel it in his gut. There was no sense of danger clawing at him. When he had first run into the store after Jun, he had dismissed her as not a threat from the get-go.

What should they do when every option felt like a bad idea? Trying to understand the prophecy was an absolute nightmare.

Nikolai shook his head. "Let's just get out of here."

Jun sunk her hands to the floor and screwed her eyes tight. Her lips murmured as she whispered something to herself. A faint wind circled around her in the still of the room. Electricity crackled, rippling outward in a ring. It rose from Jun and swarmed from her in all directions, moving beyond her. Energy pulsed through the store, stretching through the walls and outside into everything.

Jun rose to her feet, shakily, as all around them the world restarted. The ever-present background hum of electricity kicked back on. The air conditioner flowed, lightly stirring against hanging products until they swung faintly back and forth.

Outside, a body slammed into the pavement. A high-pitched shriek, cut off mid-yell.

Nikolai gripped his blade tighter. That was the twin, one half of the duo who came prowling into Jun's store. If deciding not to end the threat was a mistake—if Jun got hurt because of his idiocy—he would never forgive himself.

Nikolai was halfway out the door when a dull boom sounded directly above them. Like a muffled firecracker.

"Shit," Nikolai said in a low voice. He stepped into the street in time to see a burst of light shoot up straight into the sky like a second sun. It erupted like a supernova.

Jun had followed him outside, looking skyward and biting her bottom lip.

"Earthquake lights," Nikolai muttered for her benefit.

The twins were gone without a trace. The streets were empty, with nothing but his memory of the sound of her body falling to the earth. He never even got a look at the other. There was nothing to distract him from this phenomenon that was lighting across the mid-morning sky.

It was a ball of brilliant light, angry, vibrant, and explosive. Like a god had reached forward and grabbed the sun out of the sky, yanking it closer. Until they were all exposed to the blinding intensity of it.

"Earthquake lights are used as a signal. It pinpoints the location of powerful magicians. They're basically a billboard announcing to every assassin in the Order that you're here. They're going to send reinforcements. They're all going to come after you."

CHAPTER 14

The third time Tessa had given the signal to go, it was clear that Nova was ignoring her. Tessa picked up a yarn ball, spinning it a full three-sixty in her hands. Again. But Nova was looking determinedly at a fountain pen as if it was suddenly the most important thing in the world.

Tessa stalked within a few feet of her sister, hissing in her smallest voice, "This is just reconnaissance. Let's go."

Nova shook her head faintly, and Tessa stalked off to the other side of the store.

Nothing was happening.

The most interesting thing that happened was that this witch—supposedly powerful and the answer to all their problems—got a phone call a few minutes ago. She had a conversation that lasted, like, ten seconds before she went back to the same thing she'd done for the past three hours. Knitting. Quietly knitting. Occasionally she would take out a spreadsheet and jot down some numbers on it, frowning.

There was no way that this was the most powerful witch in the world.

Xochitl must have gotten the name of the store wrong or something.

If she was the most powerful witch in the world, this girl could be living in the lap of luxury, easy. She could bend people to her will. Become the master of huge corporations. She could be a politician, or quietly controlling the world behind the scenes of things. She wouldn't be knitting. Working at a small indie craft store in downtown Hayward.

The door to the store was yanked open and a muscular man launched into the store.

Holy shit.

Tessa recognized that cruel scowl. The piercing blue eyes that had locked on the witch.

His picture was circulated in meetings, used as the background for the dart boards and effigies for as long as Tessa had come into her power as a witch. Now he was here in the flesh.

Nikolai Visiliev.

Tessa's heart started to race, and every hair rose on her arms and the back of her neck.

He'd killed so many of their kind. Now he was here in the same room. Breathing the same air as Tessa and her hotheaded sister.

He was locked on his target. The witch who was their only hope to stop the destruction of the entire world.

Time seemed to slow to a crawl as Tessa turned to her sister, mouthing, "No."

But it was too late.

Nova had already clenched her hands into fists, tight. Until her fingernails broke through the calloused skin of her palms. Drawing her lifeblood, calling on her magic.

The winds swirled, gathering force and speed until craft

supplies got ripped off their displays, turning them into projectiles.

Tessa saw it like it was in slow motion as Nikolai's focus shifted away from Jun to her sister.

Without thinking about it, Tessa shifted into her own magic, calling on the light within her. She reached inside of herself and pulled tight until a cloud formed around her, whiting everything out. Anyone within the cloud would not be noticed. Would not be remembered. Cautiously, Tessa walked over to her sister.

The cloud slipped around her, fading away at the edges, threatening to dissipate entirely. It only worked if the people within the cloud were unobtrusive enough not to draw attention to themselves. Nova was doing too much, drawing way too much attention to herself. The attention of a murderer.

Tessa watched in horror as Nikolai drew out his blade, ignoring the witch completely, setting his sights on her sister.

Nova was fully under; the dark power had taken her. She'd described it like a rush. Like a surging, swirling confidence rising over her head. Like her brain had turned into a fizzy drink and the bubbles and sugar high were swirling around her head. It was a bit like being in daze. Or being in love. Being drunk. Or being incurably stupid and reckless.

Her sister coiled wind into another one of her pressurized tornadoes and hurled it at Nikolai as he drew his blade.

Another weapon mentioned in the bi-yearly safety meetings in the coven. It was meteorite iron. That blade would pierce through magic like a heated knife would cut through butter, and Nova had as much of a chance of withstanding a direct hit from it as a chihuahua facing off against a Siberian tiger.

Tessa screamed helplessly as Nikolai hurled the blade—though Nova managed to contort the wind, knocking the table upwards, trapping the blade within the wood. Tessa pushed her way through the wind, whether her sister wanted it or not. Whether she was under the dark thrall and control of her magic or not, Tessa was going to grab her and get her out of this.

Though no one could see her—Tessa was essentially invisible—that didn't mean that she wasn't really there. She arched her arm, shielding herself from the boxes, packages, yarn balls that hurtled across the room at hurricane speeds as she forced her way across the store.

Then she felt it. Like all the electricity within the room was singing. Vibrating, faster and faster. Tessa had no choice but to stop before that electricity called to her, singing to her, singing to the particles within her blood, coaxing all of them to join her, to come with her, to surrender to their siren call. Like the fiddler of the story, leading the children of the village away with his songs. The magic pulsed within her like a living thing.

Her blood was bursting with the memory of the power of it. Washing over her and drowning her in a wave. She jerked, forcing herself to break off the hold of the magic at play before it sucked her in. Before she lost control of her own casting and dropped the invisibility entirely.

Tessa turned to the short Asian shopkeeper.

The witch.

Funny. She had somehow entirely forgotten that this girl was supposed to be the most powerful magic wielder in the world, sometime during the three hours of watching her do a whole lot of quiet knitting. The witch had her hands to the ground, and Tessa could feel the magic pulsing, radiating up the girl's arm. Flowing up from the well of energy from the earth itself.

The witch snapped her eyes open and in the next moment, Nova was in the air. Thrown bodily out of the window of the store, crashing through the glass.

Tessa reached out to her, helpless and silent. She couldn't call out to her or risk drawing notice to herself, magic or no magic.

But before Nova had even fallen to the ground, magic rippled up again, coiling around the store, around Tessa, and then rippling outward in a wave. Covering and coating everything.

Everything stopped.

The wind that had howled through the store was utterly silent.

The craft supplies whipping about and crashing into everything stopped.

There was a faint ringing in Tessa's ears.

What the hell was this? It was like time stopped, but how? That wasn't possible.

Was it?

The silence was broken by sniffling as the witch that caused all of this started to cry.

It was only when Nikolai walked over to the witch with hearts in his eyes that Tessa realized the extent that they screwed all of this up.

CHAPTER 15

Victoria shuffled through her cards nervously—not channeling power through them, merely rearranging them. The coven had assembled for another emergency meeting, and Victoria pressed herself deeper against the cracked leather. Maybe if she was out of the way, she wouldn't think about the fact that she had dredged up all of this drama—drama that wasn't going away.

Samuel rubbed his eyes furiously with the distinct look of someone who was not getting enough sleep at night. If any. "You were supposed to just go in and take a look."

Nova crossed her arms furiously as she tilted her chin up. "At first she wasn't showing any signs of power at all. Nothing. We had to be sure."

"So you made a tornado? I've seen the earthquake lights mentioned on Twitter, Facebook and Instagram. We're all going to have to lie low."

"You don't understand." Nova scowled. "Visiliev was there. He came to the store. He went straight to the witch. I thought he was going to kill her, or us."

Victoria dropped a card at the mention of Visiliev's name. She reached down with shaky hands to retrieve it and frowned when she noted the Star card lying faceup. She shuffled it back into her pile.

"What the hell was Visiliev doing there? Isn't he supposed to be retired? Xochitl, didn't you say he was retired? Can you double check?"

Xochitl ripped her headphones off and let her huge blue bubble of chewing gum pop before she nodded. She closed her eyes as she channeled her brand of magic, seeking the correct current of information within the energy of the internet.

"Then what? After Visiliev got there and the tornado. Then what happened?" Samuel had both of his hands in his hair and looked to be on the verge of ripping it out.

Nova's mouth snapped shut as she turned to look at her sister.

The rest of the coven turned as well, heads pointing to the far corner of the room.

The witch in question, Tessa, was wide-eyed. She was introversion personified. Myers Briggs type INTP and everything. Definitely used to letting her sister steal the spotlight. Victoria could relate to that.

"Okay, this is going to sound crazy." Tessa took a deep breath, as if bracing herself. "The witch, Jun. She stopped time."

There was complete silence in the coven. The only sound was Victoria's card shuffling.

Samuel's mouth hung open. He closed it and opened it, doing his impression of a drowned fish, before regaining his train of thought. "What do you mean stopped time? How is that... That's impossible."

"I don't know how else to explain it. Everything was

moving around in the whirlwind and then—nothing. It all just stopped, instantly. Things froze and went silent. Even Nova. She was hanging in midair. Completely still. I've never seen anything like it. It didn't feel like real-life anymore. It was like being stuck in a picture, or some scene from a movie."

Samuel began pacing, muttering his thoughts out loud. "The magic involved with time travel. That has to be a powerful affinity with both light and darkness." He shook his head, looking back at Tessa. "Could you tell what her Take was?"

"I couldn't see anything."

"The darkness probably doesn't require a physical Take from her, then. Must be something mental. Did she look..." Samuel didn't finish his sentence. He didn't need to. They had all seen what happened when dark magic drew too much from the wielder's mind. Some began to lose their grip on reality. Some witches even became cruel and had to be persuaded to give up dark magic or lose their place in the coven. Persuading them didn't always go over well. Dark magic was addictive.

But Tessa shook her head. "No, Jun seemed fine. Totally normal."

Samuel shook his head. "That doesn't make any sense at all."

"Then the Ancient One arrived."

Samuel paused his restless pacing and stepped closer to Tessa. "How did she summon the Ancient One?"

"Uhh. There was no summoning. He just sort of showed up." Tessa blinked rapidly. She took to being in the spotlight much like a deer trapped in headlights.

"Okay... How did the witch react?" Samuel rubbed his forehead. After all the prep work that went into their summoning, Samuel did not look pleased that the Ancient One just showed up for this unknown girl.

"She gave him a hug."

"A hug?"

"Yeah." Tessa cleared her throat, unnecessarily. Her eyes flicked to the door, as if she was imagining an escape from the conversation. "Then he put the store back for her. Fixed all of the damage from the tornado."

"That sounds like a mighty big ask. What did she have to sacrifice for that?"

"Uhh... nothing. There was no sacrifice. The Ancient One just sort of did it. I think he likes her," Tessa muttered.

"He performed powerful magic for this witch, and your working hypothesis is that he did it because he likes her?"

"Uhh, yeah. That's what it looks like. It sort of looked like he hugged her back. As much as a rabbit can do that."

Samuel was holding on to his forehead like this situation was giving him a massive headache. "What about Visiliev? Did he fight the witch? You didn't mention anything else about him."

"Umm. I think that the two of them are involved."

"What's that supposed to mean? Involved? Like business partners?"

"Not exactly." Tessa turned beet red, across her cheeks and all the way to the tips of her ears. "I saw them kissing. It looked like he's in love with her or something."

For a moment, silence hung over them as the words sunk in.

Visiliev, killer of witches, was in love with a witch?

Victoria stopped shuffling entirely. She had pulled the Star card at the mention of Visiliev's name. There was no denying it.

But how could that be?

The quiet had a heavy presence, like a fog drifting all around them and weighing them down.

Then everyone started talking at once.

"Kissing? What in the actual fuck is going on?"

"Visiliev and his family have killed more witches than any other hunters. There's no way any witch in her right mind..."

"So what does that mean? Are they dating? How could they be dating if she has magic?"

"I'm pretty sure Visiliev is a psychopath, or a sociopath... The one that doesn't feel any emotions. He can't be dating someone."

"So our plan can't really involve Visiliev's girlfriend, right? Because that's crazy. That's asking to bring Visiliev's wrath down on all of us. This mission sounds more and more like a death wish."

"Everyone quiet down," Samuel ordered.

The room fell quiet, though people still exchanged worried looks. Tessa took the opportunity to creep to the back of the room.

He didn't say anything at first, as he stared off into space as if in a daze. Samuel tapped his index finger in a quick pattern against his skin.

"Victoria," Samuel said.

Victoria shot up, almost dropping a card into her lap.

"Hey, I need you to do another reading. We need to find out if this witch is really necessary. What will happen if we try working without her."

Victoria nodded absently and tuned the rest of the room out. She took a deep breath, her focus drowning out the muttering of the rest of the conversation of her coven.

"Are you sure that Visiliev's status is unchanged?" Samuel said in a voice that sounded far away.

"Yes! I've checked it three times already." Xochitl's voice was only as loud as a whisper, as all noises began to fade.

"Then what is he…"

Victoria tuned it all out until all she could hear was the rustle of her own breath.

It was just her. As if the room in front of her was blacked out. In front of her was the Ikea table and the worn leather of the sofa under her.

This time the draw was simple. The answer would be a yes or a no. All based on whether she associated positive or negative emotions with the card picked. She let the question fill her mind.

Can we stop the end of the world without the most powerful magician?

Victoria placed her hands on the cards. She felt the warmth, the flicker of energy calling to her. The slish and drag of shuffled cardstock.

She drew a card. Though it was more as if the card had reached out to her, tugging at her.

Victoria flipped the card and revealed Death. The cold darkness within the sockets of its skull locked on her. The armor worn in the card fell away as the creature swelled to a gigantic size, towering over her.

Grass blades pierced her feet as the night sky bloomed above her.

The cracked leather of the sofa was gone.

The voices of her coven members were gone.

Victoria was alone with the massive bones of the Gashadokuro. The skull opened wide, grinning down at her, until the grin stretched wider and all she could see was the rotten jaws of it all around her.

The teeth came crashing down. A wall of splintered

bone, snapping shut. Until all she could feel was the sharp pressure of it on her neck.

"Victoria!"

She was brought back to herself. She looked up at Samuel, eye-level with her, arms on both of her shoulders, his face white as if he had seen the monster too.

Was she crying? Victoria felt wetness on her cheek. She pressed a shaky hand there. She stared blankly at the red on the tips of her fingers, smearing down across her palm.

What had happened? That was just a vision. Visions were supposed to be all in her mind.

Tessa came rushing over to her, brushing cooling white magic along her neck and the back of her head.

"I'm guessing that's a no from the cards, then." Samuel closed his eyes, nodding. As if the decision was out of his hands. "We'll have to let things cool down a little. Try meeting with the witch again in two days."

Victoria swallowed sharply. Samuel didn't get it. None of them understood what they were facing. She took deep breaths, forcing herself to calm down enough to say it. She had to let them know.

"Without her, the world is going to come to an end."

CHAPTER 16

Marco sharpened the edge of his dagger against the whetstone. Others used honing steel or more modern sharpeners, but Marco had always found the repetitive motion therapeutic. Using the whetstone also gave him more control over the edge of the blade. Knives were the most important tool in their arsenal.

Nothing else was quite as effective in stopping a magician as meteorite iron. He didn't quite understand it. His bunkmate in training had said that it was because the substance was from another planet and that a magician's energy was drawn from earth. But that sounded like a bunch of hocus pocus to him anyway.

The Order limited the distribution of meteorite iron. Sharpshooters had a limited number of bullets. They could either pull the metal from the corpses, like Logan had resorted to, or face early retirement. Same with arrows tipped with the metal, though not that many assassins used arrows anymore. Though the Order controlled a fair amount of stock on the material, the fact remained that meteorite iron would always be limited in quantity.

From the other room, Marco heard a distinct ringtone. He looked up sharply, pausing his sharpening.

"This is Giovanni speaking."

Marco strained to hear the voice of the operator. The voice of the man directing things behind the scenes.

The snatches of conversations he heard were enough to jolt him into full attention.

"New development in your territory... distinct media coverage of earthquake lights in downtown Hayward."

"We're close to tracking down Ryan." Giovanni's footsteps paced.

"Prioritize Hayward. We got signs of a magician capable of mass destruction."

This new development threw a wrench in their plans after they had spent days narrowing down their current target, Ryan. Wherever he was, he was close. Just out of reach. Giovanni was like a shark in the water, smelling blood and latching on to the smell of it.

"All right. Got it."

He hung up the call and stepped back into the main room.

"Any problems, boss?" Marco asked as casually as he could.

"New priorities. We're going to start patrolling downtown Hayward."

"Anything interesting out there?"

Giovanni shook his head. "Seems like it is just some small business and a few restaurants nearby."

"That's such a waste of time." Marco muttered.

Why did the Order have them sniffing around little shops now? Just when they were finally narrowing in on Ryan.

He thought he'd spoken the words under his breath, until Giovanni replied. "Not necessarily."

Marco raised an eyebrow.

Did the head honcho have a trick up his sleeve?

Giovanni held out a sleek case, snapping it open. "This just came out from Headquarters. A new way to flush out those who deal in the supernatural. Magicians won't stand a chance against it." From inside, Marco caught a glimpse of a metallic sheen he was deeply familiar with.

Marco leaned in to get a good look.

Wait.

Was that a needle?

CHAPTER 17

Nikolai grabbed Jun's travel bag and slung it over his shoulder. Jun's room was filled with a mountain of soft knitted stuff that Nikolai vaguely remembered as pastel colored from when he had run in to save Jun from a shadow creature. Now all of her knitting and everything else appeared to him in shades of gray.

Jun had a highlighter in her hand, and she was currently marking parts of her pet's care routine. Nikolai clenched his teeth together to stop himself from snapping at her that they had to move. The prophecy said that killers were coming for Jun in three months... and now it was exactly three months later.

It might have taken him up to the last moment, but Nikolai had finally convinced Jun to go.

A weight dropped in the pit of his stomach as he thought about it. They were supposed to come for her. Today.

Let them come for her. Let the killers come all they wanted.

Nikolai and Jun were going to run.

The tickets had already been purchased. He'd booked the first available plane out to the Seychelles when Jun finally responded to his question—where do you want to go —with, "I don't know. Somewhere sunny, I guess."

Images of the Seychelles looked plenty sunny when he'd Googled the place.

It was also over ten thousand miles away.

"Done," Jun muttered.

She walked over to the three-tiered cage that took up a third of the space of her bedroom, reaching out to her fluffy rodent.

"Hey, Pickle Berry," Jun crooned as the walking fluff-ball jumped straight into her hand. "Mommy's going to have to leave for a little while, but I promise I'll be back soon. Mr. Dawson promised that he's going to take good care of you." She gently kissed the chinchilla's fuzzy head and placed him back into his cage.

"You got everything?"

Jun's bags felt suspiciously light. Didn't girls overpack for these kinds of things? What was this filled with, yarn? Not that it mattered; they could buy anything they needed as long as they were out of here. Far from whoever it was that wanted to cause Jun harm.

Nikolai and Jun piled into Old Faithful, Jun's junk Nissan, an ancient car that was held together by patch jobs and prayers. Nikolai drove as fast as the car could go, approximately a few miles over fifty miles per hour. They were four blocks away from Jun's house before Jun shot up, straightening.

"My binder!"

"Your binder?"

Jun groaned. "I left it at the store. I can't believe that I left it at the store."

"It'll be there when we get back," Nikolai reassured her.

Jun shook her head. "I can't leave it."

"You can't leave it..." Nikolai echoed. "What do you mean you can't leave it? Of course you can leave it." Nikolai stared blankly at the road in front of him. What was in the binder that was so important, now of all times? Her business plan? Why did she have no sense of self-preservation? It wasn't like she was going to be able to sell any yarn if she was dead. They had to *go*.

"It has my passport in it."

Shit.

"What? You told me you had your passport!"

"I usually keep it in my travel bag, but it's not there... I needed a picture of my passport for a bank thing, and my scanner's at the store."

Jun still had her driver's license; they could use that to travel within the continental United States. Would the East Coast be far enough away? They could stop there and order a new passport. Though, getting a new one sent over could take months, and even fake identification took weeks to get all the specialized watermarks and security features that would pass inspection.

Her shoulders hunched forward dejectedly as she bit her lip. "It'll just take me a minute."

This was a terrible idea. Jun had no idea what a killer could do in a minute. Professionals wouldn't even need a minute. It only took a few moments to slash and break something that was never meant to be broken. Some things, once broken, weren't possible to fix again.

But a minute now would keep them safer for months. Who knew how long they would need to be on the run?

Cringing inside and cursing, Nikolai turned Old Faithful around, heading to Get Crafty. He parked outside of the store, ignoring Jun as she claimed, "I'll just be a second," heading right after her. He wasn't going to leave her side for a second.

Jun jammed her hand into her backpack shaped like a teddy bear, rooting around through the balls of yarn, before grabbing the fluffy charm attached to her keys.

She hastily unlocked the doors to Get Crafty. She flung the light switch on and jogged across the room. Nikolai was right on her heels.

The room felt cold and sterile. The lights flickered in static before turning on. The store, far from feeling like a place of crafts for fun activities, felt tense. Like a held breath, or a watch wound up too tight with no place left to tick, just mechanically pulsing, tightening and tightening. Uselessly.

The pressure was bearing down on the two of them, like Jun was under a magnifying glass, with all the force of time and fate and the prophecy itself watching.

Jun stopped at a drawer under her counter and pulled out three binders. She rapidly flipped through labeled spreadsheets with highlights and graphs. All organized with tabs and sheet protectors. She dug her hands into thick folders, reaching into the pockets.

"Not with the inventory files," Jun muttered, pressing her hand to her forehead. "I could have sworn I left it here. It's just so weird. I know that I left it right there. Unless I put it with the..."

Nikolai stood stock still, glancing at the door, his eyes flicking to the windows, as Jun rummaged. She yanked papers out of organized folders, scattering them across her glass counter, and hurriedly sifted through them.

Nikolai tightened his hold on the car keys. Instinctively, he reached for the hilt of the weapon he had hidden in an inner panel of his sleeve. The tip of his index finger touched the cool metal of his blade.

Jun gasped, and Nikolai's attention shot to her. Adrenaline pounded through his veins, and he shifted his stance slightly, ready for a fight.

"I got it." Jun beamed, holding her passport tight with both hands.

Nikolai sighed in relief. "Good. Jun, we got to go."

Jun swiped her hand across her forehead as she nodded. "Okay," she agreed in a quiet voice. "Let's get out of here."

Just then the entrance door to Get Crafty jangled.

Nikolai had been distracted for a moment, his attention fully on Jun's bright smile after her chaotic hunt through her binder. He had stopped watching the door, their only entrance and exit out of here.

"I'm sorry," Jun said, jamming her passport into her pocket. "We're actually closed today..." Her voice trailed off when she recognized her customer. Blonde hair, arranged in coiled ringlets. Manicured fingers and a sleek polished outfit. Heavy make-up that almost hid the blank look on her face.

Suzie. Jun's old college roommate.

Nikolai hadn't noticed the emptiness in her eyes before. Excused her as being tired, he'd written her off as an old acquaintance the first time she'd visited Jun's store. How could he have forgotten that this girl had once been under the influence of magic? Just a handful of months ago, the creature of smoke had leaked through her pores into her skin and taken control of her.

The influence of dark magic wasn't something that ever truly went away. He shouldn't have forgotten it.

Suzie strolled into the center of the room, her eyes half-drawn like she wasn't fully in control of her mental faculties. Like she was under the influence.

Nikolai drew his blade and stepped to the side, blocking Jun from view.

Why hadn't they locked the door?

Well, Nikolai had stupidly believed Jun when she claimed that they were only going to be a second.

But Suzie stopped inside of the store and then turned around. She put her back to them, partially hidden in the shadow of a display case. Standing still as stone, surveilling the door. Like a gargoyle.

Nikolai turned and watched, following her line of vision. Outside, through the display windows, Nikolai saw another familiar face strolling down the street. Hands in his pockets, as if he didn't have a care in the world.

That customer waltzed into the store. His grin widened when he saw Nikolai, and he nodded to him.

As if it was beneath the veil, the grin dropped, and Nikolai saw shadows form across the man's face that elongated his smile into long pointed teeth, rows and rows of them in a mouth that seemed stretched far too wide.

Ryan, Nikolai recalled the name. *What the hell do you want with my girl?*

Unlike Suzie, Ryan was not frozen, watching the scene. Ryan headed straight to the rows of craft supplies and started rummaging between the items like he was any old customer.

What the hell was he doing?

What was his angle? Why pretend to shop?

Nikolai crowded closer to Jun and raised his blade defensively.

Having a person to protect changed things. He was used to fighting offensively, when now he was focused on the vulnerable figure behind him. Jun, who was the target of these people. Jun, who was barely strong enough to open a jar of pasta. Jun, who had just looked close enough at the expressions of the people who had walked into her store and realized that these weren't customers, no. And she was no longer safe. Jun gasped softly.

Damn it.

But how do you fight against a woman standing stock-still and a man who was pretending to shop, holding a pair of plastic knitting needles in his hand?

"Jun," Nikolai murmured in a low voice.

"Yeah?" Her voice quavered.

"Stay behind me. Stay close."

He felt Jun step closer, pressing herself tightly against his back. She shook faintly.

"I'm not going to let them get anywhere close to you. They'll have to get through me."

Nikolai felt her nod against the back of his shirt.

Then Nikolai took a step, eyes locked onto the man who was pretending to be shopping. Jun stepped with him, with her small palm holding his shirt in a death grip. Cautiously, Nikolai led the two of them, edging his way out of the store, facing away from Suzie, who remained locked in shadows, almost directly in the middle of the room. Taking a slow path, the long way around, far away from the dark magic man pretending to shop. Ryan was capable of something dangerous. The scent of ozone clung to his clothes as if it was imbued in him. Nikolai slung one arm protectively across Jun, holding her close.

Nikolai and Jun were almost to the front of the store

when the entrance chimes sounded off again. Four well-built men walked in, men that certainly weren't interested in craft supplies. Men that Nikolai recognized—a full team of assassins from the Order of Saint Christopher.

Fucking damn it.

Had he gotten this all wrong? Were the killers after Jun members of the Order this entire time?

"Nikolai?" a familiar voice called out.

Nikolai recognized those dark curls and rosary around their leader's neck. This was Giovanni. Nikolai had helped their team about a year back with a magician who'd done some nasty work with illusions. Giovanni was on the more religious side compared to the majority of the Order, but he was a good fighter. Honorable man. Definitely by the book. Just about the last person that Nikolai wanted to see in his illicit magician girlfriend's craft store.

"Giovanni, what are you doing here?" Nikolai stiffened, casually sizing up the four of them. The men seemed well rested. Not on high alert. They were looking about the store. One man—Nikolai thought his name was Marco—looked blatantly bored.

"Order work. We're scouting out the area. Did they send you as backup?"

"I'm retired," Nikolai admitted automatically, and immediately regretted it.

Why hadn't he lied? Said he was escorting Jun out for testing or something so the two of them could high-tail it out of there?

His fear for Jun's safety was clouding his judgment.

"What are you doing here? Did you hear about the earthquake lights?"

"Thought I'd pick up a new hobby." Nikolai looked

around at the crafts as if he had a casual interest in knitting or something, as he searched for Ryan's location.

That dark magician would be the perfect thing to distract the assassins, as soon as Nikolai could point him out. It was the perfect excuse. Nikolai had gone in there to kill Ryan and was trying to save Jun—who was obviously nothing but a civilian.

Except that Ryan was no longer wandering the store clutching a pair of knitting needles. He didn't seem to be anywhere. What game was that fucker playing, coming in here and vanishing?

Leaving Nikolai's excuse about needing a new hobby as nothing but an obnoxiously suspicious thing to say.

Nikolai took a deep breath. He'd get Jun out of here. Just had to be casual. Pull her out of the store, into the car, and race down the road to the airport. "Well, good luck on your search. I won't bother you."

Nikolai grasped Jun's hand firmly with his own. Squeezing her palm reassuringly. Reminding her that he was here for her. He wasn't going to let her get hurt. He didn't care that he knew these people. It didn't matter that it was four against one. He would fight to get her out. He wasn't going to let them touch her.

"Sorry, Nikolai, but I can't let you leave just yet." Giovanni nodded at his team. The tallest man, Logan, dressed head to toe in camouflage, moved to stand in front of the door, his bulky arms crossed.

"We've got a plane to catch," Nikolai growled, biting against the rage, the utter need to tear these men apart.

"Someone with you, then? Care to introduce us?"

Panic over keeping Jun safe was twisting him up inside; he was playing this out all wrong, and Jun was about to pay the price.

"I can vouch for her, there's no need for that. It's just my girlfriend, Jun."

"We've got our orders." Giovanni held up a thin needle-like instrument. "No one's exempt. Not even you."

"What the hell is that?" Nikolai could tell from the deep metallic sheen of it, the luminous flecks of silver catching the light, that the testing tool was made from meteorite iron.

"New technology, just developed a month or so ago. It just takes a prick. Non-magic folks barely feel a thing."

Hell, no.

"How do you even convince people to take this... test?" More importantly, how was Nikolai going to convince this goody-two shoes to let them go without taking it?

"We tell them the truth. There's a deadly outbreak in the area. This test will save lives and help those who are infected to get treatment."

"This is a terrible idea. You lot don't look anything like medical professionals. People just let you prick them with that? Is it even sanitized?"

"Some require a bit more persuasion." Giovanni sighed.

Nikolai's eyes twitched at the thought of these muscular guys 'persuading' Jun to get tested.

It might not have any direct effect on Jun if she wasn't actively using magic. But what if it did? What if the Order pricked her skin and revealed her magic? They'd take her.

Nikolai shifted uncomfortably as he realized that he had no idea what they did with magicians they took away.

Protect the magician. Others come to kill her in three months.

He didn't need to know. The prophecy already made it clear what they would do to her if they got their hands on her.

Simple logic wasn't going to work on them.

This group followed the protocols religiously. But he

could try social pressure. Let his reputation within the Order work for him.

"I retire for a few months and the whole West Coast Division falls apart." Nikolai injected his tone with as much scorn as he could manage. "I'm calling the operator to let him know that this testing procedure is a security hazard. Civilians are going to start asking questions. Do you want to make the Order public knowledge?"

Nikolai tightened his grip on Jun, half-dragging her behind him as he stepped by Giovanni—if he could blow past the men fast enough, the exit was right there.

Giovanni held his arm out, blocking their path.

Behind him, one of the members of his team shifted, eyes flicking between the two of them, unsure.

"Nikolai." Giovanni's voice lowered in warning.

"Are you serious right now? Move." Nikolai deepened his tone as he stepped right into Giovanni's space.

Giovanni narrowed his eyes. With one three-fingered motion, he signaled his team.

There was a brief moment of hesitation as his men struggled with moving against a fellow Order member, but this was a group used to following their leader's orders. Marco and Demetrius circled around Giovanni, approaching Jun from each side. At the exit, Logan clicked off the safety on the rifle slung across his chest.

His little threat to call the operator would have probably worked on a different team. But not with Giovanni.

Nikolai clenched his nails, feeling as they bit into his calloused palm. So this would all end in a fight after all.

"I'm not letting you use my girlfriend as a guinea pig for your untested technology. Get away from her." Nikolai backed up, blocking Jun from the others.

"That's against Order protocol and you know it, Nikolai."

Giovanni called over to his team. "Hold him down; there's a chance Nikolai's been compromised."

"You think I've been what?" Nikolai said in disbelief as the two bulky men each grabbed him by the arm—which was obnoxious, but fine. They wrestled his arms in a tight hold, bracing for his resistance with all of their body weight. Neither of them made eye contact with him.

He tensed as they moved Jun away from him. He only relaxed when they tightened their grip on him, ignoring Jun, who had been shaking faintly behind him. As long as their attention wasn't on Jun, it didn't matter what they did to him.

In fact, now would be the perfect time for her to escape. If only there was a way for him to signal to her to run without drawing attention to her.

Against his arm, Nikolai felt a sharp prick.

A dull ache radiated down his limbs, and a headache formed across his forehead and at the back of his eyes.

Ow. *Barely feel a thing, my ass.*

The room bloomed into color for one bright moment before settling back into dull grays.

Nikolai blinked, momentarily disoriented. He hadn't even realized that meteorite iron would have an effect on him. Hadn't connected the dots that the thing that Jun's rabbit had done to his vision—that was magic.

"He's clear," Giovanni announced, nodding at the pinprick on his arm.

Nikolai mentally rolled his eyes. Their little test didn't even work. "Happy now?"

"Sorry, it's just protocol."

"This isn't protocol, this is insanity," Nikolai muttered. "All right, get off me."

"You got it, as soon as we test your girlfriend. Then the two of you will be good to go."

Nikolai grit his teeth. None of these assholes were going to touch her. Not over his dead body.

It was four against one. Odds that weren't that different from going against a magician, especially one capable of Level Two damage. Nikolai had taken down plenty of magicians in his time.

The air around them felt pulled tight. Heavy with all the tension in the room, weighted down by hard stares, thick with testosterone. The weight of indecision, the weight of prophecy, the weight of this one single moment, one hair-trigger away from erupting into chaos or tragedy. With Jun's life held in the balance.

Time itself was as sluggish as a sleeping beast that was lethal enough to rip them apart once it fully awakened.

In one whip-fast move, Nikolai jerked, breaking Marco's hold and tossing him into Demetrius. He pivoted, standing in front of Jun, blocking her from view. Nikolai slipped his finger against the handle of his dagger, poised for the moment Giovanni's team moved against Jun.

Giovanni opened his mouth—to give orders, to tell Nikolai to be reasonable, it didn't matter. Events were spiraling out of Nikolai's control. He didn't see a way for the day to end without bloodshed.

All the light in the room began to dim.

Leaping high into the air, Ryan launched himself at the team. As he moved, his body distorted into something less and less human. His hands elongated into claws and his jaw split open into rows of teeth.

All the dark from all the lost places—the forgotten depths that lay behind everything—surged to Ryan from every corner of the room.

The very air around him twisted into night.

It transformed him into blackness as deep as a void. As shadows converged around him, it looked like darkness itself was attacking.

Voices spoke all at once.

"That's our target."

"Marco, at your three o'clock."

"Get in position."

Marco, closest to Ryan, hurtled his dagger through the air in a hammer grip. The blade pierced through the air until it glanced off the edge of a display hook, changing the angle. The dagger was too fast and headed straight for Jun. No time to push her out of the way.

Without a thought, Nikolai moved. He pivoted, covering Jun with his own bulk.

Nikolai grunted as he felt the quick hot pressure like a punch to the ribs. He fell to his knees as all the blood flowed out of his head, leaving him dizzy, and the world exploded back into full colors—the pastel of yarn balls, the red leaking around the handle jutting out of his side. The vibrant purple of Jun's knitted hat and the soft pink of her lips that moved oddly sluggishly, like in slow motion. He thought he recognized the shape of his name on those lips.

He felt himself fading.

As Nikolai probed the wound at his side, feeling exactly which ribs the blade pierced through, he knew. His eyes widened as he looked at Jun.

His beautiful girl.

Dark doe-like eyes, she was all sweetness. She was safe.

If he'd done nothing, they would have killed her.

If he could turn back time, he would do it again. All over, saving her again and again.

He felt his system go into shock, felt his body weaken with catastrophic blood loss.

He might be dying, but he'd always known that might be a possibility. What he couldn't be prepared for was falling for Jun—falling for her and leaving her behind and defenseless in a room full of assassins.

CHAPTER 18

One minute, Jun was struggling to find the binder that she knew without a shadow of a doubt was in the drawer of her store, and the next thing she knew, all hell broke loose.

First with the customers who were not customers.

With the stress of opening her business out of the way, once Jun saw that unfriendly face again, she was painfully aware that nothing about this moment was normal.

What the hell was going on with Suzie?

Now that she wasn't distracted by her sales, or lack thereof, Jun recognized that blank look on Suzie's face. She'd had that same expression when she had gone under the control of the dark. It was the expression of someone not fully under their own power. She might not have those all-black demonic eyes, where the darkness leached across the corneas like a demon; she might not have quite the same halted and jerky zombie movements. But Jun knew. She wasn't quite in control of herself anymore.

Her old college roommate slunk into the shadows, staring motionless at the front door.

The other one walked around the store, and Nikolai tensed at the sight of him. That was when Jun knew that she had made a mistake.

Why did I have to forget the stupid passport in the first place?

That was only the start of the shitshow.

Jun froze when the assassins entered her store. She swallowed as it felt like her throat was tightening up on her.

Assassins that recognized him. They addressed Nikolai by name.

Jun watched the conversation go completely downhill as the team of assassins insisted on testing them. This wouldn't be a test like trigonometry; they were out for her blood. They were looking for her and they were about to find her.

What would happen to them if they found her?

What were they going to do to her?

She didn't have to ask; she knew what they were planning for her. She'd known for all those months when she'd carefully pushed that knowledge out of her mind.

Nikolai reached back and gripped her hand reassuringly, and it helped her breathe again.

At least until the other assassins pulled out a cruel looking needle. It was too long and too sharp for a simple test, no matter what he was saying.

Did they really think that any normal person was just going to sit still and let strangers stab them with their test shenanigans? Had they met normal people before? This was ridiculous. It was insanity. There was no way that they managed to talk people into this.

Besides, by the way that Nikolai shifted at the sight of the thing, it was likely to work.

Once the assassins pressed that against her, she was toast.

She had to do something.

She couldn't just sit here, placidly, like some damsel needing to be rescued. Not when she could do something about it.

Determination settled around her, fluttering through her chest, pushing her chin up and her shoulders back. She could do this.

Fears slid away as cold clarity settled over her. Energy hummed within her in response. Ready and waiting for her.

Jun swallowed as she turned her attention inward. Tuning out the conversation around her.

Quietly, subtly, she gathered the magic around her. She wouldn't do it quickly. Grabbing all the energy she needed rapidly left energy thick in the air. It was as noticeable as walking through mushy soup.

Instead, she pulled the magic toward herself slowly in little sips. Swirling it around herself in little drags of power, letting it slip in, filtering in like sunlight through the window blinds rather than a fast supernova dredged up all at once. It was delicate work, like knitting a scarf, taking tiny pulls of yarn and weaving them together. And like if she was knitting, Jun was overlooked. It happened all the time. The pull of yarn, little by little, and suddenly someone would exclaim that she had almost completed an entire scarf. Or a blanket or something. She pulled the energy of the magic within herself and felt all her anxiety melt away.

All she had to do now was stop time around the two of them. Just for her and Nikolai. She had to phrase it carefully to the magic.

This wasn't safe. She needed more time. She needed a minute to get out of this. Just her and the man sent to protect her, not the others. The others were just there to hurt her.

Jun pulled the magic to herself, weaving the energy together in her mind like a tapestry.

A shadow leapt up into the air over them. As she looked up to figure out what it was, Nikolai grabbed her around the middle, pushing her away.

The push loosened Jun's grip on the magic, and as it slipped free, time stopped.

Jun recognized the utter silence as everything froze. Gone was the hum of electricity, the conversation. She could hear her heartbeat. Each one of her breaths was a loud rush of wind.

Her hands shook as sharp jolts of electricity pulsed down her limbs. She clenched them into fists. She had to get a hold of herself.

Behind her, something thudded and crashed to the ground.

Jun whipped around, turning to find Nikolai's gaze locked on her. She got to her feet, moving toward him. *All right, now Nikolai and I can get out of here.*

Jun sprinted forward three steps before she noticed something was wrong.

Nikolai wasn't moving. He wasn't reaching out to her. He wasn't making any snarky complaints about how she almost got the two of them killed. His gaze didn't change to follow her movements. He was stopped in time, along with every-thing else.

She faltered in surprise before rushing over to him.

"I'm sorry, I'm so sorry. This has to be some kind of mistake. Maybe I can fix this," Jun said. She placed her palm on his cheek, feeling the faint stubble on his chin. Feeling the warmth of him. He was right there, yet he might as well have been thousands of miles away.

"Wait a minute," Jun muttered, then rolled her eyes because she would be waiting for more than a minute.

Nikolai was hunched over in an awkward way, reaching at his side. Jun took a step around, and her hand drifted down from his chin. At first, she stared at it blankly, not understanding what she was seeing.

A handle jutted out of the side of his ribs. Nikolai was frozen, pressing his hand against it.

Jun gasped and clasped a hand against her mouth. His injury was frozen in place, but it was bad. His blood had already started to seep out between the fingers at his side.

This was all her fault.

When had that even happened? Where had the knife come from? Jun hadn't even noticed it. She had just stopped time. Was she just a little too slow? What was the point of stopping time if she was already too late?

As her gaze drifted back to his face, Jun noted the faint lines of tension.

She couldn't try to bring him into the stopped time with her. She didn't have any tools to heal him. That was a knife wound in his ribs. If it hit anything important, it could kill him.

But she couldn't leave him—Nikolai was surrounded by a team of men who wanted to hurt him.

Abruptly her vision became blurry, and the corners of her eyes began to feel wet.

Jun grasped Nikolai's face in her hands.

"I'm sorry," she whispered. "I'm so sorry. This is all my fault."

Jun pressed a kiss against lips that were warm, yet completely stiff and motionless. When she broke away, she heard someone mutter a curse.

She had heard something before as well. Something had fallen. Something large. She had thought it was Nikolai.

If he's frozen, then what did I just hear?

Who is stuck in time with me?

CHAPTER 19

What the hell?

He was going crazy. There was no other explanation.

Everything had just stopped. Sound had stopped. Movement had stopped. Every single member of his team, other than him, was frozen—even Logan, who was locked in place mid-sprint, with neither of his feet touching the ground. According to his watch, Marco had wasted at least a minute staring at him in slack-jawed surprise.

Marco stepped closer to Giovanni—he'd know what to do. Marco waved his hand in front of Giovanni's face as if he was saying hi.

Nothing.

Marco went as far as to touch Giovanni's nose. The sensation was off. Gio's nose was clearly warm, like he was still alive, but it felt immovable. The cartilage there should have been a bit more flexible.

Looked like he was on his own, then.

Come on, focus.

Marco shook his head at himself. They were in the

middle of a fight, there was a shadow creature capable of Level Two supernatural damage. Possibly even Level Three: catastrophic damage. A monster that had leapt out of nowhere. Yet, the first thing he did was boop his leader's nose. What did he think he was doing, poking noses in the middle of a catastrophe?

This situation was clearly magic, though like nothing he had ever seen before. Marco had to figure out how to protect himself.

What had happened to his blade? He'd thrown it at the shadow creature right around the moment everything went sideways. The last he had seen, the knife had glanced off one of the thin metal display hangers and gotten thrown off of course.

"Damn." Marco winced when he located his blade. It had lodged right between Nikolai's ribs.

No.

No, no, no.

Marco felt cold deep in the pit of his stomach, crawling down his spine and across his limbs until it slid across his mind, numbing him with horror. Within him, his gut tightened as the same thought spiraled through his mind, reiterating over and over again.

What have I done?

He held his hand out to mimic the angle of the blade and swallowed nervously. There was a good chance that this knife had hit Nikolai right in the heart. This wound could kill him in minutes.

That was not what he had intended at all. This wasn't supposed to happen.

He clutched the back of his neck, shaking his head.

Fuck.

Marco pressed his lips into a hard line. He had to get

control over himself. There was nothing he could do for Nikolai trapped in this magical anomaly.

What would Giovanni do? Did he even have to ask? Giovanni would find the magician and force him to reverse the damage. Maybe Marco could do something similar and force the magician into cooperating.

What if it's already too late?

Marco took a deep, steadying breath. His guilt was not helping anyone.

He'd be able to call an ambulance as soon as he could break free. All anyone could do then would be to hope for the best-case scenario that the blade somehow missed anything major and that Nikolai would be all right.

First things first. He'd have to figure out how to get out of here.

Marco swallowed down the massive lump in his throat.

His eyes were drawn to sudden movement. The girl, Nikolai's girlfriend, looked around, eyeing the exit in short, jerky motions.

She wasn't frozen either?

Was she the magician?

She approached Nikolai and spoke to him as if she expected him not to be stuck in place. Marco saw her real-ize. Her look of horror as she held Nikolai's face with tears in her eyes, whispering to him.

The girl tensed, looking around the room wide-eyed. Her gaze locked on his and she backed away slowly. Nervously.

She didn't seem to be a magician. Timid little thing. Pretty, too. Nikolai was a lucky guy. *Not lucky, dumbass, he has a knife wound. Because of you.*

Marco walked up to the girl with both palms raised to prove that he was unarmed.

"It's okay. I'm not here to hurt you."

"Are you unarmed because that's your knife?" The girl pointed at his meteorite iron blade in Nikolai's side.

Marco clenched his eyes shut for a second as he toyed with the idea of denying it. "That was a mistake."

"You call that a mistake?" She was staring at him like he was an idiot. "A mistake is spelling a word wrong or taking a wrong turn. Showing up late to the meeting. What you've done, that's called murder."

"I wasn't trying to kill him." Marco rolled his shoulder. He shifted his weight from one leg to another, uncomfortable under the weight of her accusations.

"What, were you throwing your knife around as a greeting? I thought the two of you already knew each other."

"No." Marco shook his hand like he was trying to dislodge the bad karma, as if he could sweep it all away under some rug with the hand motions. Where it would cease to be a problem. "I was trying to get the shadow creature."

"So you've gotten my boyfriend killed because you were trying to stab a shadow?" The girl was clenching her fists as she cocked her head at him. She gave him a look that screamed, why are you this stupid? She shook her head. "What creature are you even talking about?"

Marco pointed over her shoulder to the corner where the creature had come from. "It looked like a mass of black clouds. I thought that it had clawed hands reaching out of it, or tentacles or something, but it was moving too fast for me to really see it."

"Shit." The girl paled, turning away from him. She was holding her arms crossed over her chest as she peered around the store, glancing at the windows and into the corners. It was like she had completely forgotten that he was here. Was she looking for the creature?

Was it still here?

Hiding somewhere?

Wait, did the girl know anything about the creature? Had Nikolai encountered something like this before and told her about it?

She took a half step closer to Nikolai. The movement seemed like an unconscious decision, seeking safety in him.

Marco winced.

Nikolai couldn't help her now.

Nikolai couldn't help anyone. Least of all the two of them.

"I don't know what to do," the girl whispered to Nikolai's still form. "This is all my fault; you were just trying to protect me." She sniffed loudly, and the corners of her eyes glistened with unshed tears. She barely mouthed the words under her breath. If it wasn't for the utter silence in the room, Marco would have missed it. "I can't stop this. If I restart time, what's going to happen to you?"

Wait. *WHAT?*

Marco had thought that she was some innocent, but this girl was a magic user all along. Giovanni was suspicious of Nikolai. Seemed like his boss was right all along for enforcing the test. Was she even really Nikolai's girlfriend? Or was she the reason he retired? Did she put him under the persuasion of her powers? Forced him to love and protect her?

This girl was no pretty little thing. She was magic—a monster running around in human form.

A magic user who seemed pathetically weak.

Marco might be getting that bounty from the church after all.

CHAPTER 20

Jun was trapped with an idiot.

It could have been worse, she supposed. She could have been trapped with someone who had better aim. An assassin who possessed more than half a brain could cause her some real problems. But at least they would annoy her less.

Jun turned at the sharp sound of a boot scraping against the tile, jolting her out of her thoughts. As he stepped toward her, something had changed in his expression. A subtle shift that was just enough to remind her that this man was trained as an assassin. It didn't matter that he wasn't as perceptive or as skilled as Nikolai. He was still built like a linebacker and was staring at her like she was a monster.

"I thought you were just some innocent civilian, and this whole time you're one of them," he snapped at her.

Jun blinked in surprise.

How had this guy made the mental gymnastics to think that *she* was the one responsible for all of this? "Do I look like a smoke tentacle creature to you? I'm not the one you're looking for—"

Jun could count on one hand how many times she'd done magic at all. Okay, maybe two hands. But she wasn't that creepy thing on the ceiling. This wasn't her fault.

"Witch," he spat out like it was some kind of curse. "Why should I believe any word that comes out of your mouth?"

Okay.

It didn't matter to him the kind of magic she did. Just the fact that she had the ability at all was enough to implicate her.

She had somehow forgotten that he was a killer more than capable of ripping her apart.

And Jun was alone here in the store with him.

There wasn't anywhere to run. She was confined in a space less than eight hundred square feet with a killer.

Trapped.

She didn't even have access to magic here. None of her magic worked right when she was trapped in time. It was as if when time stopped, it acted as a barrier that resisted most of the supernatural things she had attempted.

Why had she taken Nikolai for granted when he was running after her, trying to keep her safe? With her protector suddenly ripped away, Jun felt vulnerable and raw.

But really.

Jun clenched her hands into fists as the man circled her, sizing her up. She glared straight back.

He was the reason why her boyfriend was dying.

He was the reason she'd spent the last three months in fear of her own shadow.

Was she going to let this idiot who had stabbed her lover take her down, too?

She obviously wasn't as strong as him, but she wasn't defenseless. There was one trick left.

Jun swallowed, closing her eyes in concentration.

Hey. I need help. Please, come defend me against this assassin.

The thought burst through her, a shining point under a wave of dark despair. As the words filled her mind, another cooler brand of magic flowed through her. Running down her limbs, like she had plunged her arms into cold water.

Jun's eyes snapped open as she felt the magic take hold. She was better acquainted with the feel of it and knew that she had done it. She'd summoned help.

But she opened her eyes to nothing. Just the face of the assassin, bringing his lips together into a firm line, much closer than he was before.

"Don't even think about it," the assassin snarled at her.

"Why are you so annoying?" Jun gritted her teeth as she backed away from him. "Wasn't it bad enough that you had to hurt Nikolai? Now you've gotta come after me as well?"

His jaw tightened and his hands clenched. He nodded to himself as if he had decided something. He was clearly making up his mind, and whatever he was deciding was not in Jun's favor. He held his hand out, reaching as he invaded her space.

She strained her ears, listening for anything. Any sign that help was coming for her. The scratch of lion claws, or the deep rumble of a pissed off predator. The rustling of sphinx feathers. Anything. But all Jun heard was the deep breaths of the assassin who narrowed his eyes at her.

The assassin lurched forward and grabbed Jun by the throat.

CHAPTER 21

Jun clawed at the hands around her neck as her breath was cut off and little black spots burst in front of her vision.

She couldn't breathe.

Pressure. Harsh and unrelenting.

Blood raced through her veins as her heart beat faster and her lungs ached uselessly. She gasped, trying to force tiny wisps of air down her throat, but there was none.

She couldn't breathe.

Her grip on her attacker's hands was feeble and getting weaker. She could feel her strength fading as she choked. Gasping uselessly for air that wouldn't come.

A cloth fluttered in the air, hovering behind the assassin.

What the hell?

She stopped her useless struggle and stared. The long strand of cotton flew like a serpent undulating through water.

Shit.

She was going to die because instead of summoning a

sphinx, she'd screwed up and summoned some kind of magic blanket.

The pressure around her neck slackened and Jun gasped. As the oxygen hit her system, she felt reborn. She took an enormous gulp of air and she could think again.

Jun pulled away from her attacker, clutching at her throat, coughing.

She got herself shakily to her feet. She had to pull herself together. Be ready to move, be ready for the next attack. But when she looked up, she saw the flying cloth wrapping itself around the assassin's head.

He batted at it, punching and pulling at it, but the cloth kept coming. Twisting itself around the man's arms, pinioning them to his body. Then wrapping, pulling tight, round and round the man's face, covering his nose and mouth. As the cloth constricted, the man screamed in terror, muffled behind layers of fabric.

The assassin forgot Jun entirely as he flailed beneath the cloth. As multiple layers of cotton wrapped around his head, the assassin dropped to his knees. Eventually he toppled flat onto his back, first thrashing about with hefty kicks, which after a minute turned into ineffective twitches.

A tiny rip appeared in the top of the cloth in the shape of a mouth. The rip opened and closed, and the thing spoke in a fluttery voice.

"What would you like me to do to him?"

Of course.

The flying blanket thing could talk. Obviously. With the way her life was going at the moment, it made perfect sense to start conversations with fabric.

"I don't care what happens to him," Jun muttered. She rubbed her throat to smooth away the sting, the sharp remnant of pressure.

"Shall I kill him?" The cloth rippled as it spoke, both ends stretched taut, tightening its hold on the assassin.

Jun sighed.

Did she really want this guy killed?

Well, he had just tried to kill her. It made more sense to kill him now rather than sparing him. She'd risk facing him again the next time he came after her.

The memory of another death flashed through her mind. Kind eyes, clouded over in pain. Spending his last moments trying to send her a warning, trying to get her to leave. This was the exact same end her father had faced—as someone stronger suffocated him. Squeezed his throat until he couldn't breathe. Didn't let up until he was dead.

No matter what she tried, Jun couldn't forget his last moments. Couldn't erase the exact second that the light went out of his eyes, never to come back.

Did she really want another death?

Jun gulped. She was being stupid. Hopefully it wouldn't get her killed. "No. Don't kill him. Just wait till he's unconscious and let him go."

The rip in the cloth curled down in a frown. "As you wish."

The cloth loosened around the assassin's face and his body fell to the ground, motionless. As still as everything and everyone else locked in this moment of time.

CHAPTER 22

Jun lifted the hand of the idiot assassin, watching as it hit the ground again with a heavy thud. He was unconscious, then. Not locked out of time like the rest of the world. Merely unconscious.

Leave him.

The thought entered her mind, unbidden, of her would-be killer waking up lost in the time between time. Struggling to survive. How long would he make it here, absolutely alone? Surrounded by other people who would never hear him? The thought of him aging. Wrinkled. Grabbing food where he could like a thief, a time bandit. Only ever existing in this moment. Until the day he died. And when time restarted, his dried out and aged corpse would turn up somewhere unexpectedly. Out of nowhere, freaking people out.

He'd deserve it. For killing Nikolai.

No. No one deserves that.

Jun stepped around the tall assassin wearing camouflage with a rifle slung around his back. *How does a guy like that walk around and not attract the cops?* Then she pushed as hard as she could against the closed front entrance.

If Nikolai was here, he'd be able to open the door.

If Nikolai wasn't injured, she could just restart time. Restart it right in the middle of a fight with the assassins sent to kill her.

If she was just a few moments earlier, if she had just managed to summon the right man into this space in the time between time, none of this would be happening.

This was all her fault.

What was she going to do?

Jun pressed her back against the door and let herself slide down to a seat on the floor. She folded her hands, pressing them under her chin, as she tried to think.

Come on, think.

There had to be something that she could do.

Wait.

The last thing that the guy said, before she stopped paying attention, was that he saw the shadow monster.

Could it be the same one?

It had to be. How many shadow creatures could there possibly be hanging around her?

Jun wasn't even completely sure what that thing was. Sometimes it came in the form of a monster—a mass, a blob of darkness that seemed to bubble over, revealing features. Sometimes, within the dark, one could see eyes, or limbs, or tentacles reaching out. But when it wasn't in the form of a monster, it looked like a little black rabbit.

She wasn't quite like the white rabbit. She was a little more elusive. A little moodier. She wasn't quite so eager to help Jun out with her problems.

Jun wasn't really sure of anything about her, except for one thing. She wasn't really a rabbit. In fact, Jun didn't even really know exactly what she was, or what she wanted. The creature had something to do with magic, and she hung around Jun. Not as openly as the white rabbit. But sometimes, even when the black rabbit wasn't making her presence known, Jun had a sense that she was nearby. Lingering.

The idiot said she was here.

What did she want?

Jun caught a flicker of movement from within the shadows on the ceiling. She narrowed her eyes, trying to see.

"Jun," the shadows whispered.

She wasn't sure if it was their actual words or if it was something spoken directly into her mind. The voice was odd. Though distinctly feminine, the voice sounded like it was spoken through male vocal chords. And it was familiar, though Jun could not recall ever hearing it spoken before. It sounded to her like a voice that she knew. A voice that she always had known.

The whisper was all the warning she got before her eyes adjusted to the growing darkness and she saw exactly what it was she was looking at.

With too many pairs of human limbs all ending in clawed points, the creature hung from the ceiling like a massive spider. The thing had a human face that grinned too widely. As Jun started, a tongue that was wide at the base and came to a pointed tip drifted out of its mouth and licked dry lips. The person hanging from her ceiling was Ryan, the customer who had come into her store and pretended to shop. Though Jun doubted that this was really Ryan—somehow Ryan and the dark rabbit were mixed together.

As the thing with Ryan's face scuttled closer on the ceiling, Jun wanted to back away. But there was nowhere to go.

Her feet felt leaden, too massive to move. She felt heavy, frozen in place as she was flooded with uncertainty. The black rabbit had helped her in the past. What was she doing now? The dark rabbit wasn't planning to hurt her.

Was she?

Jun had about a moment to brace herself before Ryan leapt from the ceiling. He didn't go after her. Instead, in a tangle of too many human limbs, shrouded in shadow, the creature scuttled closer. Until it was right in front of her. There was no escaping it now.

Jun took a shuddering breath to brace herself. "Who are you?"

"Why ask questions when the answer is already known to you? You know me." The sound of her voice seemed to drift away. Escaping back into hiding and flitting into corners within moments of being uttered.

"We've just never spoken before." Jun felt like she was being chastised for forgetting the name of an acquaintance.

"Yes." The dark one lifted an arm to look at the palm of her hand, extending and curling the fingers. "This form has proven useful, allowing me to communicate in a language that you will understand."

"Why are you here?" Jun swallowed, forcing down the lump in her throat. "What do you want from me?"

"Have you ever wondered how the gifts you've been given worked?" Her mouth stretched wide, reaching from one edge of her face to the other. Within her mouth, darker shadows formed the suggestion of pointed teeth. "No, my dear, you weren't one to ever question your gifts. Always assuming that they were freely given. I can see how you made the mistake, as your magic came at a pittance."

"Does that mean that..." Jun turned the rabbit's words over in her mind, trying to make sense of them. Trying to get at the things that the creature *wasn't* saying. "Does magic have a price? I didn't know. No one ever told me."

"You, who studied business in an academic institution, should know better than anyone that everything has a price. When have you ever gotten anything handed to you? No, dearest one. You earned every last thing in your life. From your academic effort to the hours you toiled in exchange for currency. Down to your skills with knitting craft, that was born from your sweat and effort. Does it really surprise you that your magic comes at a cost as well?" Her eyes gleamed with mirth.

Was this part of a plan or something to catch poor little magician Jun unaware? What did that smile mean? Why did Jun feel like she was walking straight into a trap?

"Are you here to collect payment for all those times I've used magic?" Jun bit her lip. She'd made earthquakes and stopped time. She'd summoned multiple creatures. Without knowing anything else, Jun could safely bet that the magic she used was as expensive as all hell. "But I didn't ask to have magic. It just happened."

"No one has any power over what body they were born into. No one chooses to be born. No one chooses how tall they end up, their athletic ability, physical capabilities, or intelligence, race, talent, or social status. But just the same, it is yours."

"So, what is it? What is the cost of magic?" Jun didn't want to know, but she needed the answer just the same.

"From others, I have taken their senses. I have eaten their sanity up, bite by bite. I have taken years from their lives, and the hairs from their heads. I have taken eyesight; I have taken the use of limbs."

A chill went down Jun's spine, and her legs itched with the need to move, to put some space between herself and this creature. She'd been playing with fire this whole time and she didn't even know it.

"So will I have to pick something to lose as well?" Jun looked down at the palm of her hands. What if she lost her flexibility? What if she couldn't knit anymore? Or if she aged rapidly... or only had a few more years to live?

"No one gets to choose; it is part of their destiny." The creature shook her head slowly. "Not even I can decide the cost. I merely accept the payment as my due."

"When will it happen? When will you... take payment?" Jun whispered.

From within the shadows, the creature raised an eyebrow. "You've already paid the price."

What? Jun hadn't noticed her eyesight fading or limbs failing. Would she notice if she'd started going insane? God, that sounded just like something an insane person would ask.

"Tell me. What did you take from me? Wait..." Jun looked off to the side where Nikolai clasped his side in pain. "Is that why Nikolai was stabbed?"

The creature's eyes darted to Nikolai. "No, that was nothing but an accident. If you had your passport with you, all of this could have simply been avoided."

Jun dug her hands into her hair, ready to rip it out in frustration. Even a magical creature of darkness was pointing out how dumb it was to forget her passport.

"No." The creature's smile grew once more. "I take your fear."

Jun shook her head. "That doesn't make any sense. I've been afraid of things all the time."

"When the possibility of magic—my magic, the stuff of darkness—when that possibility whirls within you, I take your fear. I take your sense of caution. Your self-preservation. Sometimes I even take your gut instincts that something could harm you. And what do I give you in return? I give you the strength to rip apart your enemies."

Jun blinked and put her hand to her temple. She had no fear? Or caution? Obviously, that was better than losing a limb or her mind or something. But having no fear sounded incredibly dangerous. Jun muttered under her breath, "Damn. Magic is trying to get me killed. What did I do to deserve this?"

"Truly, your accusations wound me," she said in a dry voice. "With every prophecy, every turn of fate, I have always, always sought to protect you."

"Sorry." Jun blushed, heat rushing all the way up to her ears. She hadn't meant to say that out loud. "I don't want to offend you or anything, but your prophecies always seemed a bit violent."

"It is because of my prophecy as well that a man like Nikolai loves you. That he laid down his own life for yours. To protect you."

"Protect me?" Jun echoed. "What prophecy?"

"I told you to run."

Jun remembered little about the events leading up to that day; it was all mixed up with the college assignments, tasks that she had to do. But she would never forget opening a fortune cookie and seeing within it the order to run.

"I didn't listen to it."

"You did as soon as you met Nikolai. You ran from him. Thus setting up all the necessary conditions for him to fall in love with you."

"Then what would have happened if I didn't pick that fortune?"

"If you had picked the light fortune, you would now be

married to that rich schoolmate of yours, likely with your first child already on the way."

"Who, Bailey? Bailey didn't even like me like that."

"That man still thinks of you, often, as the one who got away. The two of you would have been very happy. But never safe, and always vulnerable. Nikolai is the direct male heir of generations of assassins. His bloodline carries the experience of thousands of years of killers. Who better to protect you?" The dark crossed her hands together. Smug. Satisfied at her choice.

Jun shook her head. It was like the veil had been ripped away, and now it was revealed that her life was a rather large game of chess and she was nothing but a pawn in it, the events in her life moved by these creatures that she didn't quite understand.

"What about the last prophecy? That killers were coming after me?"

"I gave you a warning. If I hadn't, you would have died. My, my." She sighed, shaking her head. "You are so quick to judge me without ever considering the danger of the light prophecy. Asking you to build a craft store—a store that would bind you to one location, one little place that would build a suspicious concentration of magic—that brought about the attention of witches and assassins alike. This store is meant to trap you until it becomes your grave. On the other hand, all I've ever wanted was to protect you."

Jun swallowed nervously. That. That couldn't be true. The white rabbit, who gave her hugs and ate her cereal. He was always quick to help her out. He couldn't be secretly trying to kill her. There was no way that could be true.

"If you aren't here to collect payment on my magic, why are you here?"

"Now, now, no need to be suspicious. I am merely here to offer you my help."

Jun narrowed her eyes. "Help with what?"

The dark creature drifted away, her form becoming more shadow and less human. She moved until she was in front of Nikolai.

One blackened finger, with nails that resembled the claws of an animal rather than the limbs of a man, pointed to the injury in Nikolai's side. "The blade struck the left ventricle of the heart and pierced into the vena cava. That wound is fatal."

"He's going to die?"

Hearing her suspicions voiced out loud made everything suddenly too real. It was as if a void had opened up, taking all the air out of the room and opening all of her veins, washing all the blood out of her brain and out of her body to puddle on the floor.

Nothing made sense anymore. This couldn't be true.

He couldn't die. This was *Nikolai* they were talking about. The man was indestructible.

But if it was the truth?

From within her core, something burned. Something that had been buried deep within her and left to fester. Now it was heated past the boiling point, taking over her.

"What's even the point of telling me that?" Jun shouted. "What does it matter? It isn't as if you can stop him from dying, take his wound away and let him live."

The dark one drummed her claws against her side, looking bored. As if she was waiting for Jun to stop her little tantrum. As if Jun's behavior was simply ridiculous.

"Of course I can do that, my sweet one."

CHAPTER 23

"You... you can?" Jun swallowed, staring at the dark one as the shadows flitted across her features, over her beaming grin, replacing the mouth of a rabbit with the fanged jaws of a predator.

There was a catch. There had to be a catch. *Remember who you are dealing with.*

"What's the catch?"

"I would never try to trap you, dearest one." The dark rabbit looked away, chin pointed high with the distinct air of someone offended by a slight against them.

"What's the cost, then?" Jun got the words out rapidly. She had all the time in the world here. Though, as she stood before Nikolai with his knife wound to the heart, blood raced through her own veins as if she were running out of time.

"The magic to undo this injury is rather complicated, seeing as the assassins wounded your lover with a metal forged from a meteor, and my magic is based on the energy of the earth. It would require me to pull the material out slowly, manipulating matter around the blade and stitching up the wound behind it, or turning back time itself, reversing the moment of…"

"Look." Jun interrupted the great magic being and her even greater sale's pitch. "Just tell me what I have to pay for you to heal him. What do you want?"

"You. The price is you."

"Me?" Jun waited to see if the dark one would elaborate. She didn't. "What do you mean by me? Are you going to kill me? How does that work?"

"Sweetheart, I would never kill you. I don't want to hurt you." The dark one laughed, exposing fangs, rows of them, all crooked and sharp. "I'm not asking for a life for a life. Nothing like that. I would simply like to call in a favor."

"So, what, after time restarts, I would have to leave with you?"

"Nothing like that. I'll call it in later." The dark rabbit placed a claw to her chin as she considered her own words. Her thick tongue moved like it had a mind of its own, winding around it. Tasting it. "Don't worry, I'll give you some time to enjoy the life you've purchased. Think of it as time to enjoy your gift."

Jun took in a shuddering breath. "If I say no?"

"Of course. That is your choice." The dark one shrugged. "Then I do nothing."

"But, then Nikolai… What's going to happen to him?"

"He'll die, of course. You will have approximately two minutes and fifty-six seconds to say your goodbyes. Perhaps less if the Order of Saint Christopher interferes again. They do like to cause their little… distractions."

Jun stepped through her store, moving away from the assassins frozen in mid-fight and back to the place where she had first used her magic. She stood in the same position where she had triggered this magic in the first place and looked at Nikolai.

Jun met his intense gaze he had directed toward her when he'd been caught up in this moment.

He knew.

He knew that he was going to die. He had to have known.

She pictured him, cold. Light gone out of his fierce eyes. All that ferocity, all those desperate kisses, strength and skill that made up the man—becoming nothing but food for the worms.

Jun's stomach tightened, and bile rose up in the back of her throat. She forced the idea out of her mind.

This wasn't fair. They had only met each other a few months ago, and they had only just started dating.

"Nikolai, why did you have to jump in front of me?" Jun whispered, wishing that her voice could reach him. It was all wrong.

"He was merely fulfilling the terms of his prophecy. He protected you. If he hadn't moved as quickly as he did, you would have died in moments. In that case, there would have been nothing that anyone could do."

"Nikolai saved me."

He'd taken a death that was meant for her.

Their relationship was still new. She knew that he loved her, and she was well on her way toward feeling the same.

Letting Nikolai die, that wasn't really a choice at all.

No.

She couldn't do that to him.

She couldn't stand back and watch another person she cared about die. Not again.

She might not have been able to save her father, but this time there was something she could do.

Jun opened her mouth and forced down the utter certainty that she was making a mistake. Yes, she was. But letting Nikolai die was an even bigger mistake. Her lips opened and froze. The words were right there—say them and he lives. Say nothing and let him die.

She didn't have a choice. Not really.

"I'll do it."

CHAPTER 24

Pressure yanked around Nikolai's side like an invisible suction cup—squeezing hard against his rib cage with the force of a giant popping a pimple.

When the pressure released, he heard the word *pop*, as though a feminine voice had leaned in and whispered it into his ear. With that sound, the colors around him all switched to gray, like someone had changed the channel on his vision.

At his feet, he heard the clatter as a standard issued Order knife fell to the ground.

Wasn't that thing just in him?

Shit. This is magic.

Nikolai peered into Jun's dark and frantic eyes, then looked her over. She didn't seem to be hurt anywhere, thank God, though her fingers were trembling just as they did after she let loose a massive blast of magic.

What did you do?

Nikolai closed the distance between him and Jun, wrapping his arms around her. Pulling her close enough against him that her arms were partially blocked by his bulk. It was a good thing that Jun was so short.

Behind him, the team of Order members yelled things to one another.

"Where the hell is Marco?"

"He's down. That thing did something to him."

Marco lay crumpled in a corner. No visible wounds, though his face was red and slightly bloated. Impossible to tell from here if he was dead or knocked out.

He was just standing. On the other side of the room.

Did Jun do something to mess around with time again?

Whatever she had done, it didn't matter. He just had to get her out of here safely.

A lone bullet fired. Loud and intense in the tight confines of the store, followed by high-pitched shrieking and a disorienting ringing in Nikolai's ears.

He crouched down, pulling Jun closer, wrapping his arms more tightly around her. He pulled the both of them under her display table, knocking it on its side, scattering yarn and stationery across the floor to form a make-shift barrier.

"Gio, watch your six!"

"It's on your left!"

"Holy Mother, are those tentacles?"

Nikolai ignored Giovanni's team, eyes peeled for an opening when he could grab Jun and make a dash for the door. For now, the fighting was too chaotic. Demetrius and Giovanni threw an assortment of knives, while Logan covered their knife-retrieval. Ryan—or whatever that dark creature wanted to call itself—darted throughout the room, faster than Nikolai could track it.

Wait.

This wasn't the only customer. Nikolai peered around the store for Suzie's location.

She was still. Stock-still and standing partially obscured in the shadows.

Her face was expressionless and unmoving, until she turned her head robotically in his direction. Suzie winked at him.

In a motion too fast to track, Suzie stood and lobbed a box of polymer clay into the commotion of the fight. The box smacked against Logan's rifle, altering the tilt of his barrel. He cursed as his shot missed its mark, embedding into the floor.

Suzie went back to being immobile, as if she had never moved from the shadows at all. Was the creature limited in how much control it exerted over Suzie? Could she only be in one place at a time?

Not that that mattered. Nikolai just had to get Jun out of here in one piece.

Should he help the Order take down Ryan? Whose side was that thing on, anyway?

Help the killers sent to come after her?

Obviously not.

His shirt was damp. Nikolai looked down sharply at Jun, searching for an injury he might have missed.

His girl clung to him tightly, and fat teardrops slid down her cheek. She met his gaze, her eyelashes wet and her dark eyes watery. "Are you okay?"

Nikolai frowned.

Me?

He touched his side, prodding the spot where he had been injured. Through a hole in the shirt, he could feel smooth skin, though he was certain that Marco's blade had pierced through his ribs. Besides the cut through his shirt, there wasn't any sign of damage. No pain, no mark, no soreness.

"I'm fine." What did she do to make that happen?

Nikolai had been healed by magic before and still bore the scars of his injuries on his flesh. Back when Jun asked the white rabbit to help him. This was something different. As if he'd never gotten injured in the first place.

Jun burrowed against him tighter.

"It's okay. We're going to get out of this," Nikolai murmured into her ear as he held her back.

"I'm sorry," Jun whispered into his shirt.

"None of this is your fault." Nikolai tilted his head, indicating the fight going on in the store. "Blame them. You didn't want this."

A store display cart crashed against their barricade, and Nikolai braced against the wood as glass shattered. Yarn balls and crocheted figures flew over the top of the table, bouncing off his back.

The man dressed head to toe in camouflage, Logan, slammed hard into the stationery aisle. He rolled to his knees in one smooth motion, scattering envelopes and decorative paper as he jumped back into the fray. He stomped on a container of glitter and left behind the sparkling outline of his footprints.

The shouts of the Order got louder. When Giovanni yelled, "Got him," Nikolai peered over the barricade.

One blade struck the meat of Ryan's thigh. The wound was far from fatal, but it was enough to push the darkness out.

Shadows leaked out of Ryan's orifices, dripping out of his eyes like tears and pouring out of his mouth like smoke. The more darkness drifted out of him, the more he began to look deflated, like a balloon with half its helium leaked out, barely floating a foot off the floor. Like an ordinary man.

"Check on their vitals; I'm calling this in." Giovanni patted at his pockets, pulling out a cell phone. He flipped it open.

"You better request a full restoration for the store," Nikolai called out.

Giovanni shook his head, lowering the phone. "We could have used your help just now."

Nikolai opened his mouth, *I'm retired* on the tip of his tongue, and stopped. No one seemed to hear him or take those words seriously. People didn't seem to agree that he was allowed to stop fighting. "You held me down and tested me for signs of dark magic," Nikolai scoffed. "If you don't trust me, don't take my help, either."

"It wasn't personal, I was just following protocols."

"I told you before that that test is a security hazard, the kind of thing that'll bring down the entire Order. If I were you, I'd look into who is behind this little invention." Nikolai noted how Giovanni's lips pressed together, and the grip on his cell phone tightened. The man had way too much blind trust in the rules; he wouldn't listen to reason.

Honestly, while disappointing, this really wasn't Nikolai's problem anymore.

Leaning close to Jun, Nikolai asked her in a low voice, "Still got your passport?" As she nodded, he took her hand.

Jun winced as she looked throughout her store. None of the inventory was in place. It looked like someone let a pack of feral children run loose through it. Plastic wrappings were ripped open, and the contents of entire aisles were scattered across the floor. Items that Nikolai had spent the last couple of months helping Jun organize meticulously.

Except the clay polymer section, which was oddly pristine. Suzie remained crouched there in the shadow of the display boxes, her expression blank to the point that it looked robotic. As Nikolai took in Suzie's face, it seemed like a switch went off in her brain. She looked about the store, startled. As if she had no idea how she'd gotten there.

Suzie pulled herself to her feet, wiping imaginary creases out of her stiff skirt. She stomped out of the store, heels crunching broken bits of plastic, stationery and yarn along the way. She slipped out the door.

Not a single member of the team even looked up as she walked out. In fact, had any of them looked her way the entire time she was lurking in her corner?

It was like they couldn't see her.

Now that he thought about it, there was something about the way the light dimmed as it touched her. Something unnatural.

Demetrius had turned the unconscious Ryan over onto his back, handcuffing his hands together. Reminding Nikolai that he had no idea what happened to the people the Order took alive. Suzie was a simple case of being in the wrong place at the wrong time. Could it have been the same for this guy? Nikolai looked away from the scene.

The shrill sound of sirens pierced the air.

The two of them had to get out before they got caught up in the reports. Before backup came around, flooding this tight space with killers.

Now was the time to go.

Demetrius was holding down Ryan, while Logan and Giovanni still huddled over Marco. With the team distracted, Nikolai led Jun out of the store.

They still had a plane to catch.

~

As Nikolai approached Jun's junk car, he found that they weren't yet alone. Someone was waiting for them. Jun's old roommate. The one who was dressed in a fashionable skirt and blouse. With her curled blonde hair and manicured nails, this woman hadn't even registered as a threat until it was too late.

Whatever she was, like Ryan, she was no longer fully human.

"Oh, so you're the reason I bought all of that art crap." Suzie kept her chin high, looking down at Jun. "I'm going to want a refund for that."

Nikolai raised an eyebrow. This girl was being an asshole.

"Yeah, yeah, that's fine," Jun agreed easily. "As soon as the store's put back together, that's fine."

"I was gone from my job for two hours because of you. My lunch break is only supposed to be forty-five minutes. You're lucky that I wasn't fired."

"Sorry." Jun cringed.

She must have been talking about coming to Jun's store and shopping under the influence of dark magic. Suzie might not have recognized how it was possible. She might have just been assigning blame wherever it was easiest. The fact was, Suzie was technically right. If she hadn't been Jun's roommate, the dark one would have never taken an interest. Would never have taken over.

"I don't know what you're up to, but you better stop it." Suzie took a step closer to Jun and her nostrils flared. "If you don't want to hear from my lawyers."

With each hateful word out of Suzie's mouth, Jun was getting more and more pale.

"Noted," Nikolai snarled.

He had a strict personal code for who he killed and who

he let live. As far as he could tell, Suzie was a victim in all of this.

But she was obnoxious enough to make him want to question his own rules.

Suzie lifted her head. "You don't scare me."

Nikolai leaned in closer, looking straight into the black pits of her eyes, straight through to the hint of darkness lurking beneath. "I should."

CHAPTER 25

The last thing Marco could recall was that piece of cloth. Cotton, coming for him. Nothing but a flimsy bit of fabric. Persistent. Cotton that smelled like old cheese and floated in the air as if it was a rejected flying carpet from a Disney movie.

Then it moved, faster than he could react, tugging tight against his face like a boa constrictor. Pulling against his mouth and eyes. All he could see was stained fabric, the individual threads of it pressed tight against his eyes. Until it was wrapped so thick that it blocked out the light. Until each breath was a fight against material that was less like something woven and more and more like a living thing, pressing against him and smothering him.

Until he couldn't breathe. There was nothing but pressure, building and building, all wrapped around him, and he was falling to the dark.

Marco peeled his eyes open to fabric over his face.

Adrenaline flooded him. Blood raced through his veins as he gasped and fought to sit upright, and the cloth—nothing more than a damp rag on his forehead—slipped off.

He could see.

He could breathe.

He was in a hospital bed.

Surrounded by persistent beeps of machines monitoring him and the stench of disinfectants. There was a pulse oximeter hooked onto his thumb, and an IV taped into the veins in his hand. Under the thin hospital blanket and itchy gown, Marco suspected that there were more tubes attached to him.

He was alive. He'd gotten out of whatever weird magic time trap he'd experienced.

Marco leaned back down against the bed, which crinkled under his weight like there was some plastic sheet thrown in there.

He'd passed out. That meant that he hadn't been there for the fighting. Hadn't taken down the magician. Meaning that he wasn't going to get any of the bounty. Only more medical bills on top of the ones he already couldn't pay for his sister.

Fucking damn it.

Marco stared at the mellow green paint on the hospital walls that was supposed to calm him down and ground his teeth together hard enough to hear the molars pop and crunch, until the sound scraped its way deep through his skull.

What was he going to do now? He needed that money. Fast. His sister was running out of time.

What if he quit? Marco mentally shook his head. There wasn't any other job out there that could bring in the kind of cash he needed. He didn't qualify for a loan that would cover all her medical bills.

Marco clenched his fists, refusing to give in. But what the hell was there left for him to do? Even if he sold one of his fucking organs on the black market, it wouldn't be enough.

The door to his room slid open and Giovanni walked in, holding a Styrofoam cup of what smelled like cheap hospital coffee.

"Good. You're awake. You had us worried for a moment there."

"How long was I out?"

"Two days." Giovanni frowned and took a sip of coffee. "What's wrong, are you still in pain?"

"No, not in pain." Not physical pain, anyway. *Damn, am I really going to have to admit this?* "But honestly, I don't know how I'm going to pay for all this."

Giovanni swirled the coffee in his cup, as if the motion would improve the quality of it. "The bounty on that Ryan fellow should more than cover it. It should already be in your account."

Marco's heart rate began to speed up, and the beeping of the machines monitoring him chimed an alarm. He took a steadying breath to try to slow it before one of the nurses burst in. Did this mean that he got his share from taking down Ryan? That guy was no small fry. He was a magician capable of deadly magic—the kind that ended in a big payday. Marco didn't want to question it, didn't want to disturb the tenuous conditions that led him to possibly get the money, but he had to know for sure. "But I passed out when you took down Ryan."

"Of course you get a cut. You're a part of this team and injured in the line of duty. You even held him off on your own back in the garage. Did you think that we would cut you out for getting taken down?"

That was in fact exactly what he had thought.

It seemed unbelievable. Could he actually have the

money? The notion that it could be coming to him, that he'd be able to get Izzy the care she needed, was suddenly too much, and Marco was dizzy with it. He wanted to shut up and run off with his riches like some possessed dragon. Not to horde it, but to sit on his treasures possessively and make sure that no harm befell it. But he had to make sure. He had to absolutely know before he could relax and celebrate.

"I was just going off what happened when we met up with Nikolai, when he got the full payout for taking down the illusionist," Marco explained, saying the words quickly. Getting them all out. He didn't want to offend Giovanni. Didn't want to mess things up at the last minute and have this prize suddenly taken away from him.

Giovanni reached for the rosary around his neck and ran his index finger down the beads, one by one. "That's different. Nikolai doesn't have a permanent team. His status is... elite. The man follows his own leads and takes down the magicians solo more often than not."

That asshole must be loaded. Good thing that he decided not to interfere in the shop. But why was he there in the first place? "It was weird that Nikolai ended up being in the same store as the magician."

Giovanni's eyes darkened and his voice deepened. "I don't believe in coincidence."

What did that mean? There was no way that Nikolai could be a magician. They had even tested the guy. There had to be something that he wasn't seeing, some solid reason why Giovanni would still suspect someone with a reputation like Nikolai's. If Marco had come to trust anything, it was that Giovanni's instincts were no joke. He didn't know if it was because of faith or whatever, but if Giovanni distrusted Nikolai, there had to be a solid reason for it.

Wait.

How could he forget? That so-called girlfriend that shadowed Nikolai—she was the reason he was in the hospital in the first place. She was the one who had enchanted the cloth and nearly killed him.

She wasn't a real girlfriend at all. She was a damned witch.

That girl had to be the reason behind Nikolai retiring. Marco had never heard of the guy having any kind of romantic partner before.

An assassin would never voluntarily date a magician. Imagine kissing one? Just the thought of it had bile rising in his throat. She had to have him under his control. Giovanni was right the entire time.

As soon as Marco was cleared to get out of here, he had to tell Giovanni what was up. He would have to figure out how exactly to break the news, as the Order had strict rules about members caught in a web of magic. If he casually mentioned that he'd gotten trapped within magic so powerful it put him in the hospital, he'd be deemed compromised. Unfit to take on more assignments. Possibly even taken in for evaluation. Obviously, he had to report this, but Marco wasn't sure if he was ready to be forced into retirement just yet.

Marco squinted at the cracked screen of his iPhone. He enlarged the text on the web browser screen carefully so that his thumb and pointer finger didn't get shards of glass stuck to them. His finger hovered over the login to his bank.

This was it. Moment of truth.

Giovanni said the money should already be in there. What was he going to see if Giovanni was wrong?

Marco had about forty-seven dollars to his name right now. Perhaps less. If his cellphone bill had been processed already this month, he might even be in the negative. His bank issued a ten-dollar fee like it was Oprah giving out new cars when he was strapped for cash at the end of the month. Seriously, it was for every little thing: when a bill was processed before his next paycheck, or when he bought food with insufficient funds, and every time he breathed slightly wrong.

Marco hit the red button. Immediately his screen switched to the loading image with the little circle that spun around and around.

"Come on," Marco muttered, bringing the phone closer to his face as if staring at the numbers would make them appear on the screen any faster.

The page loaded in sections, as little rectangles of color and information appeared in full behind the shattered glass.

Marco stared at the numbers, completely numb. He let the phone slide out of his hand and onto the hospital sheets as he stared into the ceiling.

It was more than forty-seven dollars. It was a helluvalot more than forty-seven dollars.

Marco let out a breath, a rush of exhaled air leaking out of him. With it, bubbles of elation rose through him like the fizz of a carbonated drink.

There was over a hundred thousand dollars in his bank account.

He'd never had that kind of money in his life. Had never even dreamed of seeing numbers so obscenely high. Marco knew that the Order paid well for high profile magicians, but this? *This*?

He lay back on his hospital bed and had to clasp a hand over his mouth to stifle the laughter that wanted to burst free.

He could pay off Izzy's medical bills.

In fact, he could do that right fucking *now*.

Marco jerked up, ignoring the rush of air in his head. He would do it right now. Marco logged in to her medical account.

Izzy's password was always a combination of her two favorite animals, and she always liked to capitalize random bits of it.

Was it capital-zebra-lowercase-monkey, or lowercase-zebra-capital-monkey? Then there was that number one and exclamation point at the end, right. Right?

It only took two tries for his overexcited fingers to type out her password correctly. From there, he flipped through the tabs to get to the big fat button with the text 'pay now' inside. This was far from the first time he'd navigated through Izzy's account to stare at her bill. Far from it. Now, though, he could finally do something about it.

He tried to press the button, but his stupid screen wasn't cooperating with him. He tapped down two more times. Was it the cracked screen? Bad reception in the room?

Marco took a deep steadying breath. This was fine. The only thing standing between life and death for Izzy was his ability to use his touch screen. He'd put off repairing it. His phones always seemed to get broken on the job. It was over a hundred dollars to fix them...

The sound in the room was off; he had been too caught up in his bank victory to notice. Where was all the beeping? The sound was nonstop in the hospital, and now all that remained was a slight ringing in the back of his head in its absence.

Marco looked up from the glare of the cell phone screen. The lighting in the room was off as well. Who'd turned off all the lights in a hospital room?

A heavy rumbling, the growling of a large carnivore, came from directly above him.

Slowly, as if he were being compelled to do it, Marco raised his head to the ceiling. Eyes, rows of them, all of varying color and sizes, gazed back at him from within a dark smoke. The black mass writhed like a living shadow, with tendrils of it reaching down for him, coming for him.

Marco froze.

Sweat dripped down his cheek, and moisture flooded his palms as his hands began to shake. His cellphone slipped out of his grasp.

Marco stared at it. A new emptiness clawed at him as his device clattered to the floor.

No.

Had it sent? Had he pressed the button?

No, please. One little press of his button, that was all that was standing in between Izzy and certain death.

No. He had the money. It was right there. It was right fucking there, waiting for her.

His gaze was locked on his phone, and for a moment he couldn't tear his eyes away.

All above him was a night sky devoid of stars, a writhing mass of darkness.

He recognized that darkness, had just recently fought against it in the craft store, recognized the limbs trapped within it that stretched out and reached for him, clawing at him. Recognized the cold tendrils of it as they latched against his skin, pressing in all around him.

Marco took a shuddering gasp as smoke-like tendrils pressed against him, holding him in place.

It was too late to scream. It was too late to do anything. The night launched at him, purging the light. He couldn't see, he couldn't feel. He was utterly locked into place as everything in the life he knew was stripped away and replaced by the void.

THE THING that looked like Marco, but was not quite Marco, stretched out his arms. Examining his hand, first the palm and then the back of it.

This new body was far from ideal. Completely lacking in magical capacities, not at *all* like Ryan.

Marco opened his mouth to speak and a wisp of a voice came out. Like a child blowing through a wand, trying to make soapy bubbles. "Hi..."

Pathetic.

But at least this one was a member of the Order of Saint Christopher. It was always good to get a body on the inside.

Besides, couldn't very well leave this one alone. Not after what Marco had done to his darling one. Pressing these filthy hands against her sweet neck. Almost ruining everything.

There was much work yet to be done.

The thing in Marco's body unlatched the pulse oximeter and pulled off the blood pressure cuff. The machines would all be flatlining if he hadn't already disabled it. With a tug, he pulled the intravenous line from his vein, releasing himself. Blood splattered out along with the intravenous line.

Shadows crept up to the dripping injury, stopping the flow, forcing blood to settle back into his veins.

Bending down, Marco picked up the cellphone that had

fallen to the floor, cocking his head at the information on the screen that his host had been so fixated on moments before.

It was the payment for a hospital bill.

Marco tapped the diminutive 'x' in the upper corner, exiting out of the page. He pocketed the cellphone as he got to his feet.

Strange, the sort of things these mortals in their disposable little bodies got themselves worked up over.

Why worry about death? It was inevitable.

Marco sighed.

So much more to do, and so little time.

What was that human expression? Ah. The devil's work is never done.

CHAPTER 26

Jun should have figured it out the moment Nikolai ignored the long winding line at the airport check-in. Irritated people were roped off in a line that snaked around in a maze, and he bypassed that entirely. But she didn't think much of it as he marched them instead to the carpeted entrance with no line and a smiling lady at check-in. In fact, Jun didn't quite understand what was going on until they had gotten onto the plane and she made her way automatically to the back. Nikolai had to call her over and point out their seats directly at the front of the plane.

"You got us first class tickets?" Jun stared at the plush, extra wide seats at the front of the aircraft like they were a foreign language. Didn't those cost thousands of dollars? For what? She could buy her own La-Z-Boy massage chair for a fraction of the cost and have it forever. It would probably be more comfortable, too.

"Yeah." Nikolai was shoving their carry-on into the overhead compartments. Once done with that, he grabbed Jun's hand and leaned into her ear to whisper, "It's too crowded back there."

Heaviness settled over her chest and down her limbs. Nikolai was still worried that something was going to happen to her. Still tense and convinced that something or someone was going to leap out of the shadows and murder her. Even though the threat had already passed.

All this time he'd focused on keeping her alive, only for him to be the one with the blade to the heart. Ripping into him and reaving him in two, cutting deep into that powerful body like he was nothing.

Jun's gaze lingered on his side. Forcing away the memory of the blade that had plunged through his skin, the blood pooling around the edges. Nikolai suspended minutes away from death.

No. That didn't happen. She'd made sure that it didn't happen. He was safe. They were both safe.

I'll do it.

Jun forced the echo of her promise out her mind. They were safe for now. She would face the consequences of that decision later.

Long after the blade had cooled from the heat of the blood it was soaked in.

Long after the hard gazes from the Order of Saint Christopher, a team of assassins, faded from memory.

Long after this plane took off, with her butt in an over-priced seat.

Besides, the dark one had made her own promises. That she would let Jun enjoy spending time with the gift that she'd purchased.

She would figure out all the rest later.

He was unblemished and in one piece, and Jun couldn't ask for more than that.

Jun was not going to think about the fact that these seats were plush and offered firm back support. She shouldn't think about how nice it was.

Jun looked away from the other customers that filed into the airplane, making their way to the back of the plane. As if she had done something wrong to them by accepting the privilege of these fancy accommodations. She had nothing to be embarrassed about. To Nikolai, it was a safety precaution. She hoped that this didn't financially set Nikolai back. She didn't want to mess him up.

Jun's face flushed in a heat that slid up from the back of her neck. What if she had put the poor guy in debt? They didn't even need the plane tickets anymore. She should have asked him to refund them. It had to be too late to refund the tickets now that they were actually on the plane, right?

Shoot.

Nikolai was retired. He wanted to be retired. He shouldn't have had to pay for this. She could make a payment plan and reimburse him as soon as her business picked up.

She'd ask him about it when they were away from prying eyes.

Nikolai, for his part, did not look away from the other passengers.

He stared down each of them, as if daring them to come closer. Daring them with his eyes to walk up to him and see exactly what would happen. Nikolai glared at them with heat in his eyes. A heat that she could feel.

A shiver pulsed down her spine, pooling into the core of her, awakening something that had long been asleep.

Jun swallowed. Wishing that she had something to fan herself.

As soon as the other customers filed into the plane, the

flight attendants curtained off the rest of the passengers. A flight attendant brought Jun a colorful cocktail with an umbrella in it and a piece of paper. Jun reached for both, confused, noting the high quality of the cardstock before realizing that it was a menu. It had several gourmet options for a complete three-course meal, as well as what looked like a complete bar worth of drink options.

What was this? Were they in a plane or a restaurant?

Well, it was too late to get a refund now. She might as well order something.

"This is pretty intense," Jun muttered, looking over the options. Did she want the roasted beet salad with macadamia nuts and lilikoi aioli for an appetizer? What the hell was lilikoi aioli, anyway? Way too many vowels for airplane food.

It was probably fantastic.

Oh! They had passion chocolate cake as a dessert option? Jun wasn't sure how passion could get added to chocolate. Did they mean the fruit, or her newfound love for airport food? It didn't matter; she was going to try it.

"The braised beef short rib is pretty good," Nikolai leaned in close, whispering into the shell of her ear. "I'll act as your taste taster when the food comes. You don't have to worry about getting poisoned."

"No. That's dumb. Why would you be able to eat something and not die from it if I would?"

Nikolai raised an eyebrow. "I have a larger body mass, so poison would impact my body differently from yours. I've also built up a metabolic tolerance to several types of poisons."

Of course he was immune to certain poison. That was totally a normal side project. What could be more fun? What better way to spend a boring Wednesday night than developing tolerance for several poisons? This assassin's Order that Nikolai used to be a part of sounded like it was *crazy.*

Well, it wasn't like he was actually going to hurt himself. Jun's killers had already come and gone. He'd paid for this trip. If he wanted to taste some of her food, the guy could have at it.

"Hey, Nikolai. This trip isn't going to mess up your retirement plan, is it?"

Nikolai was many things—he was incredibly street smart, and knowledgeable about things like killing bad guys and whatnot. But did that knowledge translate into managing his money going into retirement? A few months back, he'd gotten her a brand new cellphone with a hefty price tag to match. The guy was in his mid-twenties. How was he supposed to have enough money to last him the rest of his life? When he was buying first class tickets to exotic island destinations? It wasn't like Nikolai went to college.

This was a nice gesture, and Nikolai might have thought it was necessary to keep her away from prying eyes of her mysterious and elusive killers. However, she could not in good faith allow Nikolai to put himself into debt. Not when she'd already spoken with the dark one. Not when she knew that the danger had passed. Did she really want to tell him the reason she knew that they were safe? The deal that she made hovered on the tip of her tongue. Jun swallowed, holding the words in, refusing to speak them. It was only going to make him stress out more.

"What? How would a trip mess up retirement? The two are supposed to go together." Nikolai frowned.

"Umm, all of this seems really expensive..." Jun fidgeted, picking at the corner of the fancy menu.

"Oh." He rubbed at the back of his neck, clearing his throat as if embarrassed. "Don't worry about it. It's fine."

"Aren't you supposed to never have to work again? I don't want to mess that up."

"My finance manager told me I could retire four or five years ago." Nikolai must have noticed some lingering frown on Jun's face, because he went on. "I never really spent anything that I earned, besides for therapy. Spent thousands on that. My father was injured in his prime and had to retire early. My brother died in his thirties. I always assumed that the same could happen to me."

Jun bit the inside of her cheek to stop herself from frowning again. She would just have to check over this financial advisor later to make sure they weren't screwing Nikolai over.

She flipped through the screen in front of her, looking at the selection of movies. It was time to see if first class was all it was cracked up to be.

Jun ordered the grilled lamb cutlets with mint chimichurri and passion chocolate cake for dessert. She put on *The Dark Knight Rises* on the screen in front of her and knitted as she watched, settling into the seat. It really was comfortable. Especially if she didn't think about the price tag associated with it. Besides, since they couldn't refund anything now, it was up to her to enjoy the flight for the both of them, seeing how Nikolai was too busy glaring at every last shadow.

&

THE MOMENT NIKOLAI got their checked luggage, he had performed an elaborate sleight of hand to pull one blade out of a hidden compartment in his luggage and slide it into a sheath panel sewn into his jacket. The movement was so quick that, besides a brief glint of a metal sliver, Jun barely noticed, though she knew he was going to do it and was watching for it.

Armed, and on the lookout for any hint of danger, Nikolai slipped an arm around her. He had a hard look on his face, casting suspicious glances about. Other disembarked passengers avoided the two of them.

Is he going to do this the whole trip? It's really getting old.

When the two of them got to the hotel room, Nikolai went straight to the mini fridge and grabbed a can of the closest caffeinated drink he could reach and popped the tab without preamble.

Was he really planning on staying up all night guarding her?

No.

She had to put her foot down. There was no way that she was going to let him do that. Not now, when the danger had passed.

Besides, she was pretty sure that she could think of a way to distract him.

"Hey." Jun took his face in between her hands, feeling light stubble on his hard jawline. "It's after midnight."

"Go to sleep if you're tired. I'll watch over you."

Jun bit her lip. "I never thanked you before." She leaned in, pulling him close, pressing her forehead against his. She took in a deep inhale, breathing him in. His eyes were focused on her with an intensity she felt to her bones. "You saved me."

Nikolai's jaw tensed as he swallowed. His fear that she was still not safe wrestled with something else. Something that burned within the intensity in his eyes. Something that

Jun could feel in her core, heating her from the inside out, pooling deep in her belly.

Her skin flushed as her heart raced. Desire pulsed through her blood in a steady beat.

"Are you okay?" Jun touched his side with one finger, tracing a light path along his ribs. The fabric of his shirt lifted up in a silent question.

Nikolai's lips parted as he took a step closer to her. In a single movement, he pulled off his shirt, revealing a heavily muscled torso with deep scars.

Jun pressed her palm against his side, feeling hot muscle that was tense under his smooth skin. He was completely unharmed. There wasn't a single mark to show that he had almost died protecting her. He was perfect.

The tips of her fingers brushed lightly across his chest to a raised scar that slashed across his sternum.

"That was from a pair of garden shears. Fighting a magician that had telekinesis." His voice was low and strained.

He held himself perfectly still as her fingers slid to his shoulder, resting on a shiny patch of skin.

Nikolai swallowed. "An acid burn. The magician had a forked tongue, scales and everything."

She let the tips of her fingers glide down his arms to a scar that cut deeply along his bicep.

Nikolai licked his lips, his breath unsteady. "When the magician I was after tried to get away, I got hit by a car and pinned against a building. Almost lost my arm."

Jun brushed her thumb against his scar as if she could brush away everything that had hurt him.

In the back of her mind, she had thought Nikolai was invincible, but he wasn't. He got hurt like anyone else. It only seemed that way because no one worked harder than him. He had put himself at risk, and he had done it for her. He had fought for her. Because his feelings ran deep.

Jun stepped closer, erasing the distance between them and placing light kisses against the marks etched into him.

"I love you." She whispered the words into his skin.

Jun could feel the exact moment when her words sunk in and Nikolai's control broke. All the tension within him, the guard he hadn't let down since the moment he'd read the prophecy about the killers after her—it all collapsed as he let himself feel.

She reveled in the heat of him as his lips crashed into hers.

CHAPTER 27

The lavish hotel room was quiet, illuminated by the rays of the moon. Soft light revealed rattan lounge sofas, potted cascade palms, and a glass patio with a beach view.

Resting within was the most powerful magician in the world. Easily the most powerful magician to be born in several generations. Not that she knew. The girl was a novice, and just beginning to awaken to the full range of her power.

She was curled around her lover, and both of them were fast asleep.

Their chests rose and fell deeply. Neither sensed the presence watching them. Neither stirred.

A large cloud drifted slowly across the moon, blacking out the light in slow increments. The shadows grew longer, and they grew more sinister.

From the space behind the ottoman, the cracks beneath the plush sofa, and all the spaces where light could not quite reach, the darkness awakened.

Swirls of black merged together. A void with hints of

something lurking within. The essence of night. All the voiceless energy of trapped souls crying out into the abyss.

The smoke-like mass drifted over the sleeping pair to look upon the scene.

The darkness smiled. Speaking in her softest voice, she said, "Don't worry, my dearest one. I promised to let you enjoy him." Coils of shadows caressed the girl's temple, smoothing a wayward strand of hair behind her ear. "Take care, sweetheart. I will come for you soon enough."

CHAPTER 28

Nikolai had been wary at first about going snorkeling. He'd asked Jun what would they do if they saw a shark? To which Jun excitedly responded, "That would be awesome." Then went on to inform him of three species of sharks that lived in the area and which one she most wanted to see.

Nikolai had stated that it didn't sound quite safe, and Jun suggested that he should stop being a spoilsport.

So they'd gone snorkeling, and there was in fact a shark, and when they broke to the surface after Nikolai had grabbed Jun and swam in a panic, Jun complained that it was just a silvertip and she'd been trying to look at it.

They'd hiked to a rock pool and visited giant tortoises. Jun had taken over a thousand pictures.

Then there was the food—breadfruit chips, grilled fish. Jun had them hunting restaurants for Octopus Chapati.

The escape to the Seychelles felt less like evading killers and more like a vacation.

It was nice.

Nikolai hadn't gone on a vacation since... Had he ever gone on a vacation?

Did the trip to Wyoming count?

His family had traveled out to Wyoming. It was to support his brother in tracking down a potential coven, but they had made a stop in Yellowstone. Nikolai and his mother had gone to see a geyser and everything.

That was over two decades ago.

Waves, illuminated solely by the light of the moon, crashed over the white sands of the beach. It was a constant roar, a cycle of water gathering, flowing, and breaking apart into the foam that trickled to their feet.

Jun was tucked into his side. She leaned into him as they walked across the sand.

She was so warm.

Her short and lithe body felt perfect pressed against him.

Nikolai felt the pull to her, like magnetism or gravity, or something coiled within him reaching out to her.

Something as simple as this walk across the sand with her felt more right than anything else he'd ever done in his life.

Nikolai stroked lightly against her forearm. "You sure you want to go back?"

Jun nodded against him; he could feel the motion of it against his shirt.

"Yeah. I'm out of yarn."

Nikolai snorted, trying to force himself not to laugh. She'd packed half a suitcase full of yarn balls. He'd thought that it would be enough to last her for months, but she'd gone through it all already.

"What happens next?" Jun looked up at him through her

dark eyelashes, and Nikolai felt something hard within himself fracture, melting down like goo.

Anything. I'd do anything you want to do.

He held back, obviously. He wasn't going to scare her. Some girls were supposed to be all about plans of wedding bells and discussions of riding off into the sunset. Moving into a decent medium-sized house with a white picket fence and two-point-five children. Anything hinting at that would probably just freak Jun out. There was no rush; they had plenty of time to figure out what would happen next for the two of them.

Nikolai shrugged, keeping it casual. "I guess we're all done with prophecies. So long as you can remember not to open up any more fortune cookies, we can get to live a quiet life."

NIKOLAI WAS HELPING Jun sort through a mountain of laundry from the trip back at her place. She was holding a load that was half her height when the doorbell rang.

"Hey, can you get that?" Jun asked from somewhere under the massive pile. She stalked off, and from Nikolai's angle, she looked like a walking stack of clothes.

Nikolai opened Jun's front door to a curly-haired girl with dangly earrings who squeaked—literally squeaked—at the sight of him, taking a step back as if she was going to bolt away.

But she didn't run off.

Flashes of light ringed her eyes.

When Nikolai closed his own eyes, he could still see it. Burning bright against his eyelids. This girl was a magician. She had a strong affinity for light magic.

She also looked like she was attempting to melt on the spot. Crawl behind a sturdy piece of furniture and pretend that she wasn't there at all.

"I know that you're a magician and I don't care. I'm not going to kill you. I'm retired." Nikolai cocked his head, waiting for her to say what she came to say. "What do you want?"

"My name's Victoria." Her voice, like her body posture, was tentative, as if it were a groundhog unsure if it wanted to come out of its burrow. An ephemeral thing trying to drift away before she even finished her sentences. "Like you pointed out, I am a magician. I was hoping to talk to Jun. Is she available?"

"She's busy. Whatever you want to say to her, you can say to me." What the hell was it now? Jun just escaped from killers like two weeks ago.

"We need her help. There's a prophecy—"

"Not our problem," Nikolai cut her off. Nope. He was not going to deal with another one of those. Not today. Not ever. He moved to shut the door, and only stopped when Victoria's eyes got wide and her face got pale.

"No. Wait! Please. You don't understand. If you don't do anything, the world is going to end." Victoria had taken a step forward—after trying to shy away like a mouse—and had her hands clasped together as if she were saying a silent prayer.

Nikolai refrained from rolling his eyes. That was completely illogical. "The world has stood for billions of years; it's not going to end without our help."

"You can even Google the date. It even has a Wikipedia page, and the Mayans prophesied about it two thousand years ago. But no one is taking it seriously. No one is doing anything about it."

A pit dropped to the bottom of his stomach. Why did that sound so familiar? Yeah, obviously the world ending would get in the way of the long quiet retirement he had planned. Obviously, he didn't want the world to end. But why? Seriously, why did it have to somehow involve Jun?

Nikolai pinched the bridge of his nose. He really didn't want to hear it. "Fine. You got one minute to convince me. What exactly is going on?"

"Okay." Victoria took a deep breath as she closed her eyes. "There's an apocalypse, coming that's nearly unstoppable. The cards are warning of everything from asteroids colliding into earth, to man-eating skeletons reawakening. It's going to happen on December 21, 2012."

ALSO BY RENÉE DES LAURIERS

Divination in Darkness Series

Assassin's Order

A paranormal 9-11 call. A secret society. What could go wrong?
When 9-11 calls turn supernatural, dispatch turns to people like
Mikhail. A member of a secret society called the Order, Mikhail
has sworn to fight against the dark powers of magic. Trained and
deadly, Mikhail must determine where his true enemies lie.
Because when witches are involved, any mystery could be his last.
Can Mikhail catch a murderer before the night turns fatal?

Assassin's Order is the urban fantasy prequel to *Magician
Rising.* Make sure to get your free copy today!

Magician Rising

Dark powers she can't control. Deadly hunters tracking her down.
Can she rip the target off her back before it turns fatal?

Jun Bear has lived with bad luck all her life. And when a professor
threatens to give her a failing grade, the college senior sees her
hopes for graduating in two months going down another ill-fated
drain. But her fortunes plunge further when an unnatural
earthquake shakes the campus and unleashes cold-blooded
assassins after her head...

Unsure what's happening, Jun finds herself facing a trained killer
intent on exposing the wielder of the dangerous magic. And when

she's provoked into revealing her unexpected new abilities, she's determined to prove her innocence before she's permanently eliminated.

Can she win over an ally and survive a bloodthirsty secret society fixated on wiping her out?

ABOUT THE AUTHOR

Renée des Lauriers is the author of the Divination in Darkness series. Renée was raised by a folk-singer and an accountant to be analytically creative. From thirteen, she played guitar and sang on stage at coffee shops. She also oil painted and wrote poetry on odd paper scraps. Besides writing, Renée has worked as an emergency medical technician and a high school English teacher. Now she lives in California with her family.

Visit Renée online at www.reneedeslauriers.com.

Sign up for her newsletter here.

www.ingramcontent.com/pod-product-compliance
Lightning Source LLC
Chambersburg PA
CBHW021333190726
48288CB00003B/1093